A LADY'S GAMBIT

"How is it, Lady Danby, that you were in a gaming hell with a gentleman I told you to avoid?" Lord Hartford demanded. "Have you so little regard for your reputation that you would throw it away with both hands?"

"Is my reputation quite gone then?" she asked quietly.

Infuriated by her composure, he replied bitterly, "It soon will be, madam, if you persist in this folly. It almost seems you deliberately do the very things I recommend you avoid doing."

"I assure you that is not the case, sir. I am not a child."

He stared at her. "What do you mean?"

"You could have told me that it would be best I not see the gentleman because my . . . my husband was involved in an unpleasant incident with him."

"You have heard about that?"

She nodded.

"Then I must apologize," he said stiffly. "If I have seemed overbearing, I assure you that I had only your best interests at heart."

Violet had been prepared for his anger and contempt, not this sudden kindness, and as he quickly left the room, her heart raced, then sank.

It could not matter what Lord Hartford thought of her! She had to keep him at a safe distance while she put her plan into action. . . .

A Lady of Fortune

MONA K. GEDNEY

PINNACLE BOOKS
WINDSOR PUBLISHING CORP.

PINNACLE BOOKS

are published by

Windsor Publishing Corp.
475 Park Avenue South
New York, NY 10016

First printing: December, 1990

Printed in the United States of America

Chapter One

Alistair Fitzhugh, the fourth Marquess of Hartford, handed his high-crowned beaver to the butler, and, after this dignitary had relinquished his burden to a hovering footman, allowed himself to be escorted to the Red Saloon where his relatives awaited him. He had not been anxious to answer his aunt's peremptory note, demanding rather than requesting that he present himself at Granville House that afternoon, and only his strong sense of family had compelled him to attend. His father had been very fond of his two sisters, and Lady Granville showed no reluctance to remind him of this circumstance whenever he proved less than accommodating. Past experience had taught him that she would remind him of his father's affection and then request him to do something decidedly distasteful. Although he had been on the Continent for the better part of the past four years, he felt reasonably certain that Lady Granville, despite the loss of her husband and her only son, had not altered in manner. He sighed as he entered the room. Life was entirely too predictable

. . . quite boring, in fact.

He bowed low over his aunt's hand, his lips scarcely brushing her fingers. "Your very obedient, ma'am," he said coolly. Then he smiled with genuine warmth at the frail figure fluttering behind Lady Granville. "And yours, Aunt Dora."

The Dowager Countess of Granville, her formidable figure encased in uncompromising black bombasine, regarded him with a steel gray eye and took immediate control of the conversation.

"You are late, Alistair. You know that I cannot abide people who are not prompt. Such behavior shows a sad lack of conduct. I often told your poor father that he was far too careless about some aspects of your upbringing."

Her acrimonious speech was interrupted by two voices speaking at once.

"No, now really, Maria, that is too bad of you. I mean—" began Lady Dora, breaking off in confusion as she caught her sister's eye.

Quiet and courteous, the present Lord Granville, only son of the late earl's younger brother, had risen to greet Lord Hartford, and he gently corrected the dowager.

"He is not at all late, Aunt. In fact, I believe that he is rather beforehand. It is not quite three o'clock, you know." He turned to his guest. "It was most kind of you to come at a moment's notice like this, Hartford."

Lady Granville sniffed audibly, but before she could resume her homily on tardiness, Lady Dora hurried into speech again.

"Indeed it is, Alistair. Most kind of you, I mean. I

told Maria that you very likely were already engaged for the afternoon, but she would not listen."

"You must keep your wits packed in cotton wool, Dora," snapped Lady Granville. "Whatever his failures with Alistair, our brother at least succeeded in impressing upon him one's obligations to family. I knew that he would come." And she struck the floor with her ebony cane to emphasize her point. The dowager by no means required the aid of a cane, having recovered from her indisposition some months ago, but its value as a symbol of authority was not lost upon her, and she used it to advantage.

Lord Hartford met her piercing gaze calmly. "Well, we are all agreed upon one point, Aunt. I am most decidedly here."

The dowager smiled at him grudgingly. "I cannot deny that you have excellent address, Alistair. Nor can I fault your taste." Her gaze swept him approvingly, surveying his well-tailored coat of blue superfine, snowy cravat, biscuit-colored pantaloons, and gleaming Hessians. "There is nothing of the manmilliner about you at any rate." And the dowager directed an accusing glance at Lord Granville, nattily attired in a lilac-colored coat adorned with very large silver buttons, a pair of exquisitely fitting pantaloons of the palest primrose, and a waistcoat striped in gold and blue.

The earl, flushing but refusing to rise to the bait, forced himself to smile and replied pleasantly, "No one could deny Hartford's good taste, madam. I am sure that it is impeccable."

The new Lord Granville was a soft-spoken, rather self-important man, and he refused to allow his aunt to rattle him. Having spent portions of his childhood and youth with his aunt and uncle, he was not unacquainted with her manner, and he now had the satisfaction of knowing that the extensive Granville estates were his rather than hers. In his new position he felt that he could afford to be generous. He had not caviled when the dowager persisted in treating Granville House as her own establishment, although he felt that in the coming months he would be able to establish her in a snug little townhouse on Mount Street. Such a change would, he felt, add substantially to his own comfort, and he did not despair of accomplishing this feat before the coming Christmas.

Lord Hartford nodded at his host gravely, although his eyes were alight with amusement. "I am deeply gratified, Granville. I would not wish for my connections to find me wanting."

The dowager again stabbed the floor with her cane. "That will be enough of your levity, Alistair. We are here to discuss a very serious matter . . . and a most unpleasant one."

Lady Dora protested unhappily. "Oh, no, Maria, surely not an unpleasant matter . . . serious, yes, but it cannot be unpleasant."

"Unpleasant!" reiterated the dowager firmly. "The discussion of my son and That Woman must always be unpleasant."

"I take it then, Aunt, that we are discussing Evan's widow," said Lord Hartford in surprise. "I thought that there was to be no mention of Evan or his wife in this house again."

"That was Granville's decision, not mine," she replied impatiently. "You must know that I could not dismiss all thought of my only son so readily. Now that Granville is dead, I need no longer honor his command. But now," she added bitterly, "it is too late to make my peace with Evan and see his face again."

"But it is not too late to make amends to Evan's widow," said Lady Dora nervously. "Indeed, Evan would not forgive us for casting her off when she very likely has no means of support."

Her sister interrupted her ruthlessly. "You know better than that, Dora. We all know that Evan did not leave her penniless. If it had not been for That Woman, Evan would not have shamed his family by taking what did not belong to him. I am certain that he did it for her."

"We cannot know the circumstances, Maria. I know that there must have been a reasonable explanation for Evan's actions," said Lady Dora, quaking at her own temerity in disagreeing with her formidable sister, but determined to see that justice was done.

Lady Granville glared at her, causing Lady Dora to clasp her thin hands together more tightly and swallow convulsively.

"Of course there was an explanation! A greedy, scheming young woman named Miss Penelope Carlton of Nowhere! She saw her chance to become the Viscountess Danby and rescue herself from obscurity! She took advantage of my boy and when she saw that his family would cast him off rather than countenance such a match, she got him to take the St. Clair diamonds! A greedy, scheming wanton!"

9

she repeated bitterly. "And if it were not for Dora chattering endlessly on about our duty to Evan's widow, I would not for a moment consider having her in this house!"

"Having her in this house?" asked Lord Hartford. "You are planning then to have her come to you here?"

"Only for the sake of a little peace. Dora will not leave the subject alone and I confess that I am curious to see just what sort of creature led Evan astray. Also," she added reluctantly as she looked at Lord Granville, "there is the matter of the diamonds."

The earl had been looking progressively more uncomfortable as the dowager had continued. He had felt no earnest desire to be present at this conference and he was feeling himself more and more an intruder. The late Evan St. Clair, Viscount Danby, only son of the earl and countess of Granville, had been his cousin, and he had visited from time to time at Granville House in London and Granville Court in Sussex, but he and Evan had not been friends. The disparity in their ages, for Bevil was ten years older than his cousin Evan, as well as the difference in their temperaments, had precluded any real intimacy. Bevil had always been solemn and a little pompous, while Evan had been a carefree, headstrong boy, wild to a fault. The young viscount had been impatient with Bevil and careless of his feelings; his cousin Alistair had clearly been much more to his taste, and he had patterned himself after this flawless Corinthian. Bevil heartily wished himself elsewhere, uninvolved in this present discussion of his tiresome, long-dead cousin.

Lord Granville arose from the red satin sofa. "If you will forgive me," he said mildly, "I have an engagement to meet with men of business this afternoon. I had, uh, quite forgotten poor Lawson until this very moment. Your servant," he said, nodding briefly to Hartford and bowing to his aunts. Gratefully, he made his escape.

"Now that he is gone, I may say it plainly, Alistair," said the dowager after the door had closed behind him. "The St. Clair diamonds belong to the earl of Granville, and that is Bevil now, milksop though he is. If Evan had lived to succeed to the title, the jewels would have been his, of course, which is why he must have felt free to take them, with no regard for the feelings of his parents." For a brief moment the dowager gave way to an uncharacteristic display of emotion and covered her eyes with her hand while Lady Dora made little chirping sounds of sympathy.

Lord Hartford frowned and leaned toward his aunt, his brow furrowed. "Then you propose to bring Evan's widow here to interrogate her about the diamonds?" he asked.

Lady Granville sat up abruptly. "Really, Alistair, you cannot believe that I am as paper-skulled as all that. Now that my husband is gone, there is nothing to keep me from inviting her here to spend some time with her relatives and I shall, perhaps, learn something useful during her stay."

"I see," he replied, regarding one gleaming boot studiously. "And what will you do, Aunt, if Lady Danby chooses to refuse your kind invitation?"

"Refuse an invitation to Granville House?" she asked in amazement. "I am sure that she would do no such thing." She paused a moment. "And if she should, it will be your duty, Alistair, to persuade her to come."

Lord Hartford raised his eyebrows. "My duty, Aunt? How is that?"

The dowager moved restively under his steady gaze. "You must know, Alistair, that Dora and I depend upon you to escort her to us."

"I? I have never met the lady, Aunt. I see no reason that the lady should consent to accompany me to a house in which she must know that she will be ill received."

The dowager struck her cane against the floor in exasperation. "She will consent to come. I have written to her in Bath, telling her to expect you to call for her on Monday next. She is to be packed and ready."

There was a full minute of silence while Hartford regarded her with eyes as cool and gray as her own. When he spoke, his voice was dangerously quiet and Lady Dora fluttered nervously.

"I was not aware, Aunt, that I had any plans to travel to Bath next Monday."

"Of course you were not aware of it, Alistair," she answered impatiently. "I have only just told you. Do not try to act so top-lofty with me, for you'll catch cold at it. Besides," she added, calling her cane into action again, "you know your duty to your family. You would do it for Evan if not for me."

"I beseech you, Alistair," said his Aunt Dora in a sudden burst of courage, "pay no attention to Maria. I knew that she would set your back up with her odious, stiff-necked manner."

Hartford watched in amusement as his tiny aunt turned toward her imposing sister, ruffling like an undernourished sparrow about to do battle with an eagle. "And don't you fly into a pelter, Maria," she said warningly before the astonished dowager could venture a word, "for you know that people hate it when you are forever ordering them about. Indeed, I don't know why Alistair even came to see us today," and here she looked at Lord Hartford with such an affectionate expression that he knew he was lost, "except that he has always been such a *very* good nephew, much better than we have deserved, I am sure."

The dowager spluttered here, but before she could break into speech again, Lady Dora leaned over and patted her nephew's arm. "And Alistair, what we have done is not *just*. After poor Evan died at Salamanca . . . so tragically," she said, dabbing at her eyes with a bit of lace, "after he died and left his poor wife alone, we *should* have had her come to us then. The poor child, left a widow after only three months of marriage. But we did not. Neither Maria nor I made the least push to go against Granville's wishes in the matter, even though I at least felt that he was wrong. So *very* weak," she sighed, dabbing again. "How I wish that you had been here, Alistair. Perhaps it need not have gotten so bad if there had been someone to intercede between Evan and his papa. But now that you *are* with us again, dear Alistair, would you please do this for poor Evan and bring his widow to us?"

Lady Dora regarded him hopefully, her lace cap a little awry after her exertions, and Alistair knew that he had been fairly trapped. He, like Evan, had always felt a particular fondness for this spinster aunt who had never scolded him for any misdeed, had smuggled gingerbread and cakes to him when he was being punished and confined to his room, and had told him stories and played at jackstraws with him in the nursery. Her affection never dimmed and, unlike her sister, she never requested favors for herself. He patted her hand comfortingly, but addressed himself to the dowager.

"I would be interested to know, Aunt Maria, why you expect a young woman of gentle birth and sensibility to come to you when you have so obviously not wished to acknowledge her existence earlier?"

"Precisely because she is very likely neither of those things, nephew."

"You know that is not true, Maria!" exclaimed Lady Dora. "Dear Evan told us that her father was a vicar and that her family was a very respectable one, although not of the nobility."

"That does not preclude the chance of her being a vulgar adventuress, Dora. Very likely we will find her a pretty face and very little more than that."

"But Evan chose to marry her, Aunt," Lord Hartford reminded her. "Had you so little confidence in him?"

The dowager sniffed loudly. "Any man is prey to a well-favored face and beguiling ways, Alistair, and Evan was too young to know his own mind. Very likely he married her in a fit of pique when his father told him that he would under no circumstances acknowledge the marriage."

Lord Hartford was silent. Evan had indeed been

14

quite young, a lad of twenty-two, and his temper had been easily aroused when his autocratic father became more overbearing than usual. Although Evan had yearned after several dashing barques of frailty, he had never paid his addresses to any of the lovely young girls who had watched him wistfully at Almack's. It was perfectly possible that the Carlton girl had been his first real romance, one that he might have recovered from nicely if his father had not been so bacon-brained in his handling of the situation. Silently he cursed the late earl. Evan had been both sensitive and volatile; he would have responded to a light hand on the reins, but his father's cow-handed methods had caused him to bolt. If Evan had indeed fallen into the clutches of a grasping female such as his mother described, it was to be hoped that the unfortunate young man had died before realizing his mistake.

"Surely you would have heard something from the young woman by now if she was merely using Evan," suggested Hartford. "She would certainly have pressed you to take notice of her if she were truly an adventuress."

"Just what I have said, Alistair," said Lady Dora with satisfaction.

"She knew that it would do her no good," snapped the dowager. "Granville made that clear enough to Evan before he left us. And aside from that, she was probably afraid that we would ask her about the diamonds, demand them back from her. Not but what they're probably already gone," she added bitterly. "They would mean nothing to her but the money they could bring."

15

"And she might well have needed the money," said Lady Dora, entering the fray with spirit. "Evan told us that the poor child was an orphan, living with her sister and an elderly aunt. We knew her circumstances, but we sat by and did nothing when Evan died."

"Granville said that the diamonds were enough to lose because of her and I agreed with him," said her sister tartly, "but neither one of us were considering what was due to Bevil as Lord Granville. Even though they were ours to dispose of if we wished to do so, the diamonds have traditionally been handed from one earl of Granville to the next. It is galling to think that such a paltry fellow as Bevil knows that my son was responsible for the loss of the jewels. If That Woman has them still, I shall find it out and eventually I shall have them back in their rightful place."

"As you say though, Aunt, they were yours to dispose of if you wished and there was no formal complaint lodged against your own son for taking them. There might be a slight problem in getting them back again."

His aunt dismissed his comment regally. "When the day arrives that I cannot hold my own with one of her kidney, I shall be ready for my last prayers."

Lord Hartford looked at her rather quizzically. "What do you expect to do with her if she comes? Lock her in her bedroom until she confesses?"

The dowager sniffed. "You are foolish beyond permission, Alistair. We shall do what society expects of us. Lady Danby," she said, pursing her mouth as though the words burnt her tongue, "Lady Danby

16

will be firmly taken in hand. When she is dressed appropriately for one of her station and has some grasp of what is expected of her as the widow of a peer, she will make an appearance in society so that everyone will see that we are indeed doing our duty by the girl. That should put a period to the malicious tattlemongers who whisper that we have ill-treated her."

"And who will take her in hand, Aunt?" he inquired drily. "You?"

"By no means. I am still in black gloves and it would be most unsuitable, as well as most distasteful. Your sister will very kindly take the girl in hand."

"Sally?" he asked in amazement. "My scrapegrace, rattlebrained sister?"

"She may be rattlebrained, Alistair," said the dowager repressively, "but there is no one in London who goes on better in the ton than Sally. And it will give her something constructive to do. It is a thousand pities that Lord Randolph was called away so soon after their wedding. He could have settled her down a bit. As it is, he is not expected back in England until Christmas."

Hartford looked amused. "I see that you are actually doing her quite a favor by placing Lady Danby in her care."

"As a matter of fact, I am," replied the dowager complacently. "I also feel that the widow might confide in Sally more readily than she would in one of us."

"And that she might possibly tell Sally about the diamonds, I suppose?"

"Exactly!" answered his redoubtable aunt. "And I knew that you would be willing to do your part in this unpleasant matter, Alistair. You can be trusted to bring her to us safely."

Alistair acknowledged defeat and bowed to Lady Granville. "Of course, Aunt," he murmured, "I shall do my best." Aunt Dora caught his eye and smiled encouragingly.

As he left Granville House, Hartford berated himself silently for giving in so tamely. What a cursed mess! If Lady Danby turned out to be the schemer that the dowager thought she was, he would be bringing such a woman to London to spend time with his own family, particularly his flighty sister, Lady Sally Randolph. They would be fortunate if the widow did not disgrace them all. On the other hand, if Evan's widow were indeed a gently bred female, he would be bringing her to London and the tender mercies of the dowager. He comforted himself that he and Sally and Aunt Dora could temper Lady Granville's astringent treatment, but in either case, it would be a bad business.

Chapter Two

Stanhope Cottage, some four miles to the west of Bath, nestled snugly beside the gently flowing Avon. Its small but immaculately kept green lawn stretched down to the river and the scent of honeysuckle and late summer roses lingered in the quiet air. It was to this secure retreat that Penelope and Violet Carlton had come after their father's death four years earlier. Mrs. Serena Crawford, their widowed aunt, had been delighted to take them in, for they provided her with company and gave her a renewed interest in life. Her late husband had been a successful sherry merchant and had invested in very lucrative shipments of furs from the far reaches of Canada. As Mrs. Crawford often reminded her nieces, their competence might have come from trade, but to her way of thinking, it was better to be the widow of a tradesman in comfortable circumstances than the widow of a gentleman who was all to pieces. Penelope and Violet, who had experienced genteel poverty while their father was still living, were strongly inclined to agree with this practical view. Although her family, including her brother the vicar, had felt that she had married beneath her, Mrs. Crawford had obviously never regretted her decision, and her nieces had ample cause to be grateful for her commonsense approach to life.

On this quiet summer afternoon, Penelope and Violet were seated in the shade of a giant oak tree, watching a small golden-haired boy playing with an elderly spaniel. The scene was a peaceful one, but the expressions worn by the two sisters were far from peaceful.

"Whatever shall I do, Vi?" Penelope asked tremulously. She buried her face in her hands and her bright hair tumbled forward like a bright veil.

Violet stroked her sister's hair comfortingly. "Do you not think, Penny, that you could go to Lady Granville as she asks you to?"

Penelope lifted her tear-stained face and stared reproachfully at her. "How can you even ask me, Vi? You know how she must hate me. And why now, three years after Evan died, should she wish to see me?" Her chin quivered and she caught her breath in alarm. "Oh, Vi, you don't suppose that she has found out about our Evan!" Her eyes flew to where her son played peacefully with the dog.

"Of course not, Penny. Who do we know that would possibly be in contact with Lady Granville?" There was a brief silence while Penelope considered this, and then Violet added hesitantly, "We haven't discussed the matter for a long while, Penny, but do you not think it might be wisest if you did tell Evan's parents that they have a grandson?"

Penelope's eyes, usually a mild blue, darkened ominously and her small chin jutted forward aggressively. "No! You know what would happen, Vi. If they knew that Evan had a son, they would come and take him away from me. They would bring him up themselves because he would be Lord Granville's heir."

Violet, disliking to upset her sister further but pressed by her own conscience, said slowly, "But that is just it, Penny. Your little Evan would be Lord Granville's heir if he knew the boy existed. Do you think it right to take that away from Evan? Would your husband not have wanted his son to take his place?"

Penelope again covered her face with her hands, shaking her head violently. "I won't do it, Vi. I know that you think I am wrong, but I will not give up my son and I know that is what I would have to do if we were to tell Evan's family."

Little Evan, disturbed by the sound of his mother's sobs, hurried over to comfort her. Penelope wiped her eyes and gathered him onto her lap.

"It would be quite another matter, Vi, if we could not properly care for Evan, but we have Aunt Serena and we need not depend upon the St. Clair family for anything. Perhaps someday, when Evan is older, I might tell them."

"Someday may well be too late, Penny. I just want you to be certain this is what you want." She leaned forward and embraced her sister. "I won't tease you any more with my questions and I will do just as you ask me."

She smiled at her small nephew, who grinned back, and ruffled his hair. "What shall we tell Lord

21

Hartford when he calls on Monday?"

Penelope did not reply immediately, smoothing her crumpled lavender skirts as Evan wandered away in pursuit of a passing butterfly.

"As a matter of fact, Vi, I thought that you might see him for me." She glanced up when there was no reply and went on hurriedly. "Aunt Serena is so plain-spoken that she might give something away to him about Evan, and I . . . well . . ." her chin quivered again, "to be honest, Vi, I'm terrified of seeing him. I'm afraid that Aunt Serena might say something that she should not, but I am certain that I would."

Violet sat looking at her doubtfully, and Penelope finished in a rush. "He does not know me, Vi. Could you not pretend to be me . . . just for that one meeting?"

"What of Bevil St. Clair? He has met you."

Penelope dismissed him with a flick of her hand. "It will not be Bevil St. Clair who is here on Monday, but Lord Hartford." Penelope looked at her pleadingly. "Please, Vi, just for that one meeting can you not pretend? You know how you have always loved playing at parts."

Violet dimpled suddenly, her dark eyes dancing with mischief. "Only this time I shall be the refined Lady Danby rather than Lady Macbeth or Juliet." She paused a moment. "I wonder what manner of man this Lord Hartford is."

"If he is anything like Mr. Bevil St. Clair, he is very much a gentleman. It was so kind of him to come to me after Evan's death at Salamanca to see if I were in need of anything. It is certainly more than

22

any other member of that family did," she added resentfully. "Of course, Lord Hartford is not a St. Clair. He is a member of Lady Granville's family."

At dinner that evening Mrs. Crawford, who had spent the earlier portion of the day in Bath, shared a bit of gossip that she had acquired there. A round, comfortable woman with a motherly face, she enjoyed company and went out more often than either of her nieces, although she pressed them both to join her. Penelope, indeed, had become something of a recluse since the birth of her child.

"You can imagine my astonishment when I heard the name Granville, my dears. I was all attention in a minute. I had been talking to Mrs. Reese and her daughter in the Pump Room when I overheard the two ladies standing next to us mention it."

She glanced at Penelope. "It seems that your father-in-law had a riding accident some weeks ago, Penny, and there is a new earl in his place. They were saying what a pity it was that his own son was dead."

Penelope grew pale at this, but remained silent. Unable to bear the suspense, Violet asked her aunt impatiently, "Yes, Aunt, and who *is* the new earl?"

"Why, the pleasant gentleman who came to see Penny, that Mr. Bevil St. Clair."

Violet turned to her sister. "And so it is done, Penny. We waited too long and now Evan shall not have his inheritance."

Penelope lifted her chin stubbornly. "It is much better for him to have his mother than to have an inheritance and such a grandmother as she must be to care for him."

Mrs. Crawford nodded. "There is a great deal of

23

truth in that. And you shall never want for anything—not while I am living nor after I am dead."

"I know that, Aunt, and I thank you with all my heart."

"Penny," said Violet suddenly, "had you thought in what a different light this places Lady Granville's letter? That she has written so soon after her husband's death might indicate that she was restrained by her husband from acknowledging you. Now that he is gone, she has asked you to come to her."

Mrs. Crawford looked much struck by this. "Quite true, my love. I had not thought of that, but it might well be so. Quality or commoner, men are ever high-handed in their dealings.

"It makes no difference," said Penelope abruptly. "Going to her would mean telling her about my son and that I shall not do. And I don't believe that she feels kindly toward me. Mr. St. Clair was too kind to say so directly when he came to see me, but he made it quite clear that neither of Evan's parents wanted to see me. I was caught off my guard when he came to call, but at least I had the wit not to mention that I was with child, kind though he was." She paused. "And the tone of her note was anything but welcoming."

She directed a glance to Violet. "It is even more important now that you see Lord Hartford for me. You are quicker than I and will say the proper thing without arousing his suspicions."

Violet looked thoughtful. "It is a shame that circumstances are not otherwise so that you might take a trip to London. Then you could decide for yourself what manner of woman Lady Granville is. And it would do you a world of good just to get away for a time."

"Just what I have thought myself," agreed Mrs. Crawford. "Neither one of you have done the things that a young girl should do. Penny married young Evan straight out of the schoolroom after only a country ball or two and has kept herself at home ever since."

"That is how I have wanted it," said Penny firmly, her hand moving quickly to the small gold locket containing a lock of her husband's hair which she always wore. "I am a widow." She rose from the table and went silently from the room.

"A widow she may be," said her aunt, "but she is too young to lay her heart in the grave and wear widow's weeds the rest of her life."

"I agree, Aunt, but she will not listen."

"Perhaps, Violet, if I took you more often to the concerts and balls in Bath, she would come, too."

"You know that she would not," said Violet quickly. "She would simply insist upon staying here alone with Evan, and we cannot have that."

"Perhaps not, my dear, but we cannot have you forever at home either, playing at whist and piquet with me. I know that you are fond enough of society, even the limited type that I can offer you, but you deny yourself for Penelope's sake."

"I am no martyr, Aunt." She paused a moment and smiled mischievously. "I for one would love a visit to London. It is too bad that the invitation is for Penelope and not for me."

Mrs. Crawford chuckled. "It is all very well to make light of it, Violet, but it is not healthy for a spirited young girl to live so much out of the world."

Violet shrugged. "We must take things as they are for the moment. I am well enough for now and things may always change."

It was simple enough to say those things, thought Violet, but quite another matter to live them day in and day out. Although she was devoted to Penelope and Evan, as well as her aunt, she often grew restless in such a solitary situation. She was a naturally vivacious and sociable girl and she chafed at the confinement that was imposed upon her. She and her aunt spent most evenings playing cards, joined occasionally by a neighbor, and Violet reflected ruefully that her only accomplishment might well be her proficiency at whist and piquet. Going into Bath with Mrs. Crawford was little better than nothing at all, for her aunt chatted cozily with a few old friends in the Pump Room while Violet wistfully watched young ladies of fashion promenading with their beaux. She did not lack admirers herself, but she found her would-be suitors decidedly unappealing.

She brushed her dark hair vigorously, trying to drive away her discontent. She would be glad when Monday and the business with Lord Hartford was over and done with. It was one thing to have dressed up as Juliet and performed for her aunt and Penelope and quite another to convince a perfectly respectable gentleman that she was someone else. Although she was confident that she could do it, she could not shrug off her uneasiness at being party to such a deception. Although she was extremely fond of playacting and possessed a lively sense of humor, Violet was normally very direct in her dealings with others. Nonetheless, she thought, brushing with greater vigor, if Lady Granville had written a mere gracious note, Penelope might have felt differently about going and such a deception would not have been necessary. As it was, however, protecting Penelope and Evan was clearly her duty.

Chapter Three

The following Monday found Violet in her aunt's drawing room, awaiting her caller with distinctly mixed feelings. She was still angry with Evan's family for their treatment of Penelope following the marriage, but in all fairness she realized that the late Lord Granville might well have been responsible for their behavior. It was true that Lady Granville's note had been anything but conciliatory, but Violet was somewhat inclined to give her the benefit of the doubt for young Evan's sake. Time would tell that tale truly, at any rate. As for the poor man who had been sent to do her bidding, Violet's heart went out to him. It was most kind of him to make the trip on Penelope's behalf and the journey had probably exhausted him she thought, conjuring up an image of a comfortable, middle-aged gentleman. She had left instructions for Maggie to serve tea shortly after his arrival.

When Maggie opened the drawing room door to admit the visitor, Violet turned toward it, her carefully prepared speech of welcome dying on her lips.

"Here is Lord Hartford, miss," announced Maggie nervously, bobbing a curtsey.

The man who stood in the doorway, studying her intently, was anything but middle-aged and comfortable. His dark hair and complexion only served to make her disagreeably aware of the cool grey eyes that seemed to be measuring her. Violet paused for a moment, waiting for him to step forward and introduce himself in a gentlemanly manner, but he continued to study her, quite as though she were an object instead of a person, she thought indignantly, no hint of warmth or greeting visible in his expression.

What a thoroughly disagreeable man, she mused, relieved that Penelope did not have to face him and determined that he would not put her out of countenance by his rudeness.

Her color heightened by his arrogant scrutiny, Violet stepped forward and extended her hand to him.

"It was most . . . condescending of you to come, Lord Hartford," she murmured, choosing her words deliberately.

Hartford, noting her flush and lifted chin with interest, properly interpreted these signs of bristling and could not resist adding fuel to what seemed to be an already crackling fire. His eyes lit in amusement as he bowed and took her hand. "Not at all, Lady Danby. It was my pleasure; I assure you that you are the one who is condescending."

Irritated beyond reason by his thinly disguised amusement, Violet's eyes sparkled dangerously as she led her guest to a comfortable sofa of striped satin. At least he could no longer be towering over her, placing her at even more of a disadvantage.

"Pray be seated, sir," she said coolly, indicating the sofa, while she chose a dainty armchair of satinwood.

"You must forgive me, Lady Danby, if I seem a trifle surprised. I had not expected anyone quite so young. I had heard, of course, that Evan married you when you were little more than a schoolgirl, but I had not realized how accurate an account that was."

Violet seethed inwardly, but managed a thin smile nonetheless. "I am sorry that my appearance displeases you, sir," she said, her tone indicating that she cared not at all.

"You mistake me, ma'am," Hartford replied. "I merely commented that your youth surprised me, not that I found you unattractive."

It was with some difficulty that Violet restrained a strong impulse to box his ears. Overbearing, odious man! A quick glance at his mocking expression made her suspect that he could read her thoughts. She forced herself to smile as she smoothed her pink muslin skirts.

"You do me too much honor, sir," she replied bitingly.

He chose not to answer this sally, merely nodding his head briefly as though in agreement, the glimmer of a smile playing about his stern lips.

"I had hoped to meet your aunt and your sister, Lady Danby. Will they not be joining us?"

"I am afraid not," said Violet with composure, acutely aware of Penelope hiding nervously in the nursery with Evan. Their aunt had been bundled

30

away at an early hour to drink the waters at the Pump Room. "My aunt had a previous engagement and my sister is . . . not well."

"I am sorry to hear that. Perhaps we shall meet another time." He paused a moment as Maggie entered with the tea tray, and watched silently as Violet poured tea for them both, appreciating the pretty domestic picture she presented, a dainty figure in a pink gown trimmed with knots of cherry-colored ribbons, her dark curls threaded with a matching band. Undoubtedly she was aware of how fetching she looked and he was suddenly irritated with himself for admiring her.

"Have you given consideration to my aunt's invitation to visit her in London?" he asked abruptly.

"Lady Granville's letter seemed more of a command than an invitation," she said drily.

"That is very much her manner, I am afraid," he agreed, a hint of apology in his voice. Violet decided not to remark upon the fact that the dowager's manner was undoubtedly a characteristic shared by others in her family.

"Still," he continued, "she would be most happy to welcome you to Granville House, as would my Aunt Dora."

"And what of the new Lord Granville? Would he welcome me as well?" she asked curiously.

Lord Hartford looked at her coolly. "Lord Granville is aware of what is due to Evan's widow. He will not be at Granville House himself for several weeks, but my aunts will do all that is necessary to make you comfortable."

"Too kind," murmured Violet. "Nonetheless, Lord

Hartford, I do not feel that it would be wise for me to accept the invitation."

"Why not?" he asked bluntly.

Disconcerted by his direct question, Violet cursed herself and Penelope roundly. They had agreed that she would refuse to go of course, but in their excitement, they had completely overlooked what reason she would give. If he were the gentleman he appeared to be, he would have accepted her answer and not pressed her.

"As I told you, sir, my sister is not well. I could not feel easy leaving her."

"Your concern for your sister does you honor, Lady Danby. Is it a serious matter?"

"Nothing more than a touch of the influenza," said Violet quickly, remembering that she had told him her aunt had a social engagement this morning, which would scarcely have been the case if her niece were seriously ill. "But she is worn to a thread and relies upon me for everything."

"I am sure that she must. With your aunt busy with her own engagements, it must all fall upon your shoulders."

"I do not wish you to think that Aunt Serena neglects us," said Violet defensively. "Nothing could be further from the truth. She does far too much for us."

Realizing belatedly that she had talked herself into a corner, Violet added hurriedly, "But I cannot allow my aunt to assume all the responsibility."

"Very commendable," approved Lord Hartford. "Since your sister is now on the road to recovery, I feel certain that your aunt would want you to have a rest. I would be perfectly content to remain in Bath until you are free to accompany me."

This was very far from being the truth, but Lord Hartford could not keep himself from saying it. To his surprise, he was enjoying himself hugely. He was not certain why she did not wish to go to London, but he had become quite determined to take her there. Had he been asked his reason, he would have replied that it was for the sake of his aunts. In truth, however, he was growing curious about Lady Danby. Confident that she would think of a reason that she could not go with him, he waited with anticipation to see what it would be.

"You are too kind, sir, I am sure, but I do not feel that I could burden Lady Granville with my presence when she is still in mourning. I am certain that she would soon wish me at Jericho, for nothing is as tiresome as feeling obligated to provide for the entertainment of a guest when one is not feeling at all the thing." She sat back easily in her chair, pleased with her improvisation.

Lord Hartford smiled at her gently. "My aunt had given some thought to that, Lady Danby. Naturally she would not want you to grow bored and, as you say, she is still in black gloves. My sister, Lady Sally Randolph, will be most pleased to have your company. Her husband is away for several months, visiting his plantations in the West Indies, and she is quite looking forward to having you in London with her. So you see, Lady Danby," he said with the deliberate air of one who is about to administer the *coup de grâce,* "you would be doing us a great kindness by coming. I rely upon your generosity to help my aunts

33

and my sister through this difficult time."

Violet looked at him with intense dislike. She was certain that her presence would bring no happiness to anyone in London, but she would appear most ungracious if she continued to flatly decline. For a brief moment she let herself think about London and how much she longed to visit there. She knew that it was impossible to return with Lord Hartford, disagreeable man! Still, if she went, she would have the opportunity to form her own opinions of Evan's family and possibly find a way of helping Penelope and little Evan. It was unthinkable that Evan's son not be acknowledged by his own family.

Her mind moved swiftly through the possible difficulties. Bevil St. Clair would be the only person that would realize that Violet was not in truth Lady Danby and Lord Hartford had said that he would be away from London for several weeks. She could simply end her visit before he returned. As for the objections of her sister and aunt, Violet knew that she was quite capable of overriding them. And she would at last see London.

She turned to Lord Hartford, who had been watching her with great enjoyment. She smiled at him serenely, extending her hand to him as she arose from her chair. "I must acknowledge the force of your arguments, Lord Hartford. I shall be most happy to accept Lady Granville's invitation."

He bowed and touched his lips to her fingers. "You are the soul of generosity, Lady Danby. I shall hold myself ready to accompany you to London whenever you are prepared to go."

"I shall be ready to leave tomorrow morning," Violet replied. Far better to do this quickly before Penelope and her aunt could marshal their arguments.

He looked at her in simulated surprise, a smile lurking in his eyes. "But what of your sister's health, Lady Danby? Do you feel that you may safely leave her? I assure you, I am prepared to place myself at your service and you may take what time you think necessary."

Violet dismissed her sister's health with an airy wave of her hand. "Although she is still not feeling quite herself, she is much improved. She will be most distressed not to be able to receive you, Lord Hartford." Far better to leave quickly and avoid any possibility of Lord Hartford and Penelope meeting. Penelope was quite incapable of dissimulation, and she would doubtless either give them away completely or sit mutely through an entire call, her eyes clearly revealing her terror. That way lay disaster.

Lord Hartford turned for a final word. "By the way, Lady Danby, my aunt wished to show you every courtesy and so she sent with me an abigail that she chose herself."

A sharp retort rose to Violet's lips, but she bit it back. Doubtless Lady Granville felt that Penelope would have no abigail of her own. Mrs. Crawford had hired an abigail who served both sisters, and for a moment Violet was tempted to reply that her action had been quite unnecessary. Her good sense conquered her temper, however, and she realized that it would be as well to leave country-bred Emma here with Penelope. It would be far too easy for Emma to give her away.

Forcing herself to smile, she replied stiffly, "Lady

Granville is all that is kind, I am sure."

Lord Hartford, hearing the irony in her tone, realized with delight that she meant quite the opposite and, bowing one last time, took himself away.

As he drove slowly back to Bath, Lord Hartford was somewhat surprised to find himself smiling frequently. His call had been unexpectedly interesting. Evan had obviously chosen a wife of spirit. A remarkably pretty one as well. He had been quite struck by the entrancing picture she had presented, a simple black-haired girl with sparkling dark eyes. No simpering miss with die-away airs either. She might be tiny, but the kitten had claws, and she would certainly hold her own in any confrontation. It occurred to him that Lady Granville might well be about to encounter someone who could outface her.

Violet's thoughts were not as agreeably occupied. She was conscious of a strong desire to teach Lord Hartford a lesson in manners. His careless amusement, poorly concealed, had done little to endear him, and she resolved that he would regret it.

When his carriage was safely out of the drive, Penelope entered the drawing room, closing the door quietly behind her.

"What happened, Violet? Will he be back again?"

Violet embraced her sister. "Yes, dearest, he will be back tomorrow morning to take me to London."

She felt Penelope gasp. "You cannot be serious, Violet. Whatever made you do such a mad thing? You cannot continue to pretend to be me."

"Of course I can," replied Violet briskly. "Nothing could be better. You could never go to them, for you would be too nervous, but I shall be able to look

36

them over properly and determine if there is any way that we can improve upon your situation."

Penelope continued to be most uneasy and when Mrs. Crawford returned from Bath, she added her arguments to those of Penelope. It was as Violet had foreseen, however; neither of them could withstand her determination to go. Caught finally in her enthusiasm, the two of them hurried about, carefully packing the clothing she had that was fashionable enough for the London visit.

Before she finally want to bed that night, Penelope came in to speak with her.

"Are you quite sure you must do this, Vi?" she asked wistfully. "We will be so worried about you."

Violet hugged her. "No need, darling. I shall have a wonderful time going to parties and seeing all the things that I have only read about. I only wish that you might be there too. If things work out well, perhaps you soon will be."

Penelope shook her head sadly. "You must not tell them about me, Vi. You will be Lady Danby. Promise me that you will not betray me."

Violet embraced her again. "You goose! As though I ever would!"

Penelope smiled wanly. "Forgive me. I know that you would not." She slipped something into her hand. "Here. You must take these and wear them. They would expect it."

Violet looked at the ring and dainty diamond butterfly brooch that sparkled in her palm. "I cannot, Penelope. Evan gave these to you."

"That is precisely why you must wear them, dear. They are family pieces and his mother would expect you to wear them."

Violet threw her arms around her sister's neck. "I will be careful with them, Penny, and bring them home to you safely."

She lay awake a long while that night, wondering if she were doing the right thing, or whether she would regret her hasty decision. Finally, she concluded that she had made the only possible choice. If no one made a push to do anything, Penelope would wither away here at Stanhope Cottage. It was time for her to reenter the world and it was more than time for Evan to be recognized as his father's heir. Violet was certain that there must be a way, despite Bevil St. Clair, for the problem to be resolved satisfactorily without Penelope being forced to relinquish custody of her son. If only she could be clever enough to work it out! Obviously, however, the first step was to go to London and meet Evan's family.

Chapter Four

The next morning Violet surveyed her reflection in the glass with satisfaction. How fortunate it was that Aunt Serena had insisted upon taking both sisters to a dressmaker in Bath earlier in the summer. Although she certainly did not have the wardrobe that she would undoubtedly require in London, those dresses that she did possess were both fashionable and becoming, and her aunt, anxious that Violet appear to advantage, had pressed into her hand a roll of bills that would be more than ample to meet her needs.

For her journey today she had chosen a simple round gown of French cambric, its only trim a high lacy frill standing around her throat and the embroidered flounces round the bottom of the skirt. A spencer of white striped lutestring and a Parisian bonnet banded in satin and topped with pink roses completed her attire.

"La, you do look a picture, miss," commented Emma admiringly, handing Violet her reticule.

"Thank you, Emma. Shall we go down now? Has

Lord Hartford called yet?"

"Indeed he has, Miss Violet. And such a handsome carriage as he has, miss! I could scarce believe my eyes when I looked out the window and saw it coming up the drive."

"I am going to say good-bye to my sister and Evan now, Emma, and I should like for you to stay with them until I am safely away. There is no reason to upset Evan by a drawn-out farewell downstairs."

Pulling on her straw-colored gloves, she led Emma down the hall to the nursery where Penelope sat on the floor playing with Evan. Bending over, she held them both tightly.

"Write to me," she whispered to Penelope.

"I will, Vi. Please take care and come back to us soon."

"I will be back before you fairly realize that I am gone," returned Violet cheerfully, straightening her bonnet and waving. Penelope watched with worried eyes as her sister disappeared down the hallway and pressed Evan close to her for comfort.

To her dismay, Violet found Lord Hartford in company with her aunt in the drawing room. He rose politely as she entered the room, and a worried glance at his unreadable expression told her nothing. Hopefully Mrs. Crawford had not had time to say anything that might betray her.

"I trust that I have not kept you waiting long, Lord Hartford," she said coolly.

He bowed. "Not at all, Lady Danby. Your aunt and I were enjoying a most edifying discussion." In response to her questioning glance, he continued. "Mrs. Crawford was explaining to me the hazards of the fur trade. I understand that her late husband was quite involved with it."

Mrs. Crawford nodded comfortably. "Indeed he was. And because of it, he left me well fixed enough that I could offer a home to my two nieces."

Violet, torn between the fear that her aunt might forget and mention Evan and irritation that Lord Hartford looked down upon them for their connection with trade, said quickly, "And we are most grateful. Not everyone is fortunate enough to have relatives so concerned for one's well-being," she added pointedly.

She glanced at Lord Hartford and the slight flush that stained his cheeks satisfied her that he had understood her slighting reference to his family.

He bowed stiffly to Mrs. Crawford. "Most commendable, I am sure," he murmured.

"Fiddlesticks," replied Mrs. Crawford. "They have repaid me ten times over by the pleasure they have given me." She turned to her niece and kissed her. "You enjoy yourself, child, and come home to us soon. We shall be lonely without you. I trust you to look after her, my lord, for she has no more idea of how to go on in society than a kitten does, and that's a fact."

It was Violet's turn to color and for once she deplored her aunt's habit of speaking plainly. Lord Hartford, however, seemed to find no fault with it and assured her gravely that he would do his utmost to guide her through the hazardous pitfalls of London society. Having made their final farewells, the carriage pulled away from Stanhope Cottage while Mrs. Crawford stood at the door, waving her handkerchief as long as she could see them.

Violet leaned back against the velvet squabs of the carriage, grateful to be safely away before Aunt Serena could put her out of countenance again. Next to her sat Summers, the starchy middle-aged abigail employed by Lady Granville. Violet was grateful for her presence, for it reduced the necessity of any but the most trivial conversation with Lord Hartford. She was all too conscious of his presence across from her and studiously directed her gaze toward the countryside through which they were passing, determined that she would be neither homesick for her family nor intimidated by Lord Hartford and his relatives.

His thoughts were much more agreeably engaged. He now had leisure to consider which added most to the beauty of a woman: a speaking pair of eyes or a certain elusive sweetness of expression. Having concluded that it was a happy woman indeed who combined both of these desirable characteristics, the subject of his reverie abruptly demanded his attention.

"Lord Hartford, shall I be staying with Lady Granville or with your sister?"

"With Lady Granville at Granville House, although you will assuredly spend a great deal of time with Sally since she will escort you to most of the rout parties and balls."

Violet's eyes sparkled as she thought of the delights that lay in store for her. "I do so look forward to attending a ball in London," she commented naively. "I hope there will be a great many. It seems as though I have been buried in the country forever."

42

He looked at her in surprise and some displeasure, having formed a different opinion of her character. It would seem as though Evan's widow had not mourned him overlong. "Is that all you care for then, balls and parties?" he inquired in a distant voice.

Violet, belatedly remembering her new identity, started to inform him that she was interested in many things, which was perfectly true, but noticing his grave, disapproving expression, could not withstand the temptation to vex him further. She tossed her head and giggled affectedly.

Fluttering her eyelashes coyly, she replied, "Of course I care for other things, Lord Hartford. I can scarcely wait to visit the London shops of which I have heard so much and to ride in the Park and show off my dresses."

Hartford looked at her grimly. "I see that I wronged you, Lady Danby. Your interests are varied indeed."

Violet saw that she had succeeded in disgusting him and silently railed at herself for her hasty temper and at him for provoking her. How horrified poor Penny would be if she could have heard their exchange. Penelope, who would still wear nothing brighter than a soft gray or lavender gown trimmed with black ribbons and who resolutely refused to go out in company. Her eyes filled suddenly as she thought of her lovely sister, once so happy, now living a life of self-imposed solitude and melancholy. No doubt Lord Hartford thought that was the appropriate behavior of a widow; more than likely he approved the dreadful Indian custom of suttee where the bereaved widow threw herself on her husband's funeral pyre, she thought bitterly. She would not allow her sister to sacrifice herself to a memory, nor had she any intention of allowing Lord Hartford or anyone else to dictate to her.

Lord Hartford reviled himself after their acrimonious exchange. He had thought Evan's widow a charming, rather innocent child until her recent remarks. Child she well may be he thought angrily, but a shallow, grasping one. It was perfectly obvious that she had no thought of her late husband as she approached his home. Her head was filled with nothing save fashions and fripperies. My aunt is quite right, he thought sardonically, men are too easily taken in by a pretty face.

They broke their journey at a fashionable posting house called The White Stag and Violet, attended by Summers, ate her dinner in the solitary splendor of a private parlor, while Lord Hartford dined in the coffee room. Violet told herself that she was quite pleased by this arrangement and, if she found the evening sadly flat, it was undoubtedly because she had contracted a splitting headache. Summers accommodatingly bathed her temples with lavender water and brought her a cup of chamomile tea before retiring to her cot in the corner of the room.

Violet's headache had vanished when she awakened, and she looked forward eagerly to their arrival in London. She was careful not to provoke Lord Hartford and he was determined to be civil, so they were quite in charity with one another as they approached the outlying areas of London.

She watched eagerly as the traffic increased and they joined company with a host of other vehicles, all manner of gigs and curricles and carts piled high with produce. The inevitable clamor of a prosperous, bustling city enveloped them; they were surrounded by the clattering of iron hooves and iron wheels, the noise of pedestrians, the bawling of peddlars. They bowled down Piccadilly, past Green Park and the Pulteney Hotel, turning towards the north on Bond Street. Lord Hartford smiled to himself as he watched her eyes widen at the sight of so many shops and the colorful throngs of fashionable loungers. They passed apothecaries and silversmiths, linen drapers and boot makers, their bow windows cunningly displaying their wares to tempt those passing by.

At last they turned into the spacious, elegant square designed by and named for Sir Richard Grosvenor. As they passed No. 44, Hartford pointed it out and told her the story connected with it. Just three months earlier, on Wednesday, June 21, the Cabinet had met at Lord Harrowby's home for dinner. Rumors had reached Downing Street that morning that Napoleon had defeated Wellington in a battle outside Brussels, and the members of the cabinet anxiously awaited official notification, fearing the worst, for even the betting in the St. James's Street clubs was on Napoleon. News of the allied nations' victory came at about ten o'clock that evening when Wellington's A.D.C. arrived from Brussels, travel-stained and weary from his frantic journey, to report to the Earl of Bathurst, Secretary for War, and stately Grosvenor Square had resounded with the sound of cheering.

Violet's face glowed as she listened. "What an exciting time that must have been!" she exclaimed.

"How I should have loved to see it happening."

Hartford's expression was remote. "I must apologize, Lady Danby. It was thoughtless of me to remind you of your sorrow."

For a moment Violet looked startled, then, remembering her sister's grief upon hearing of Evan's death at Salamanca and her renewed mourning when the battle that had brought them their great victory reminded her again of his loss, her vivid little face darkened.

"Yes," she replied evenly. "It was a very sad time for the families of those who died in battle." And she fell silent as the carriage pulled up in front of one of the square's four-story, brown brick houses.

Lord Hartford glanced at her, puzzled by her curiously contradictory behavior, and then attempted to cheer himself with the thought that he was about to turn her over to his aunts, whose problem she would then become. Oddly enough, he derived small comfort from this. Indeed, he felt rather guilty as he led her up the front steps and through the door that the butler was holding open for them.

They were informed by Ruffing that Lady Granville and Lady Dora had gone for a drive in the Park, but were expecting Lady Danby and Lord Hartford to join them for dinner. Hartford, exasperated by his aunt's high-handed methods and determined that she should not dictate to him again, told the butler to convey his apologies to his aunts, for he had a previous engagement.

"I shall do myself the honor of calling upon you tomorrow, Lady Danby. I am sure that my aunts will do everything possible to make you feel welcome."

"I have no doubt of it," replied Violet mendaciously, suddenly wishing herself back in the security of Stanhope Cottage.

He watched her silently as Summers led her upstairs to her room, followed by a footman bearing one of her trunks. It occurred to him that she looked smaller than she had seemed in the carriage and somehow friendless and he was immediately annoyed with himself for noticing.

Had she known his thoughts, Violet would have been surprised, but she would have concurred with them heartily. As Summers began unpacking things, Violet looked around her new room and wondered what manner of madness had seized her to lead her into such a crackbrained scheme.

Nonetheless, what was done was done. There was no use in crying over spilled milk. Soon she would be meeting Evan's family and she would have to carry it off as best she could. Undoubtedly Lady Granville would be a dragon, but perhaps there was some hope for Lady Dora. Lord Hartford's references to her seemed affectionate and she sounded like a pleasant enough person. Strangely enough, Violet found herself wishing that Lord Hartford would be present at dinner. At least he would be a familiar face, even though he would probably conduct himself in the most odiously high-handed manner possible. Determined that she would not allow herself to be thrown into the hips, Violet resolutely turned her mind to the serious business of selecting the proper dress for dinner.

Chapter Five

The dowager tapped her cane impatiently and asked her sister sharply, "Well, where is the girl, Dora?"

The two sisters were seated in the drawing room before dinner and Violet had not yet put in an appearance although Lady Granville had sent word that they were awaiting her downstairs.

"I should imagine she is still dressing for dinner, Maria," replied Lady Dora.

"How long can it take the chit? She knows that we are waiting."

"I daresay that she is nervous, Maria, and you know that one never is quite as quick as usual under those circumstances."

Maria, who had no nerves, snorted derisively and brought up another grievance that was rankling. "I should like to know what Alistair was thinking of when he told Ruffing that he could not sit to dinner with us tonight."

"I rather imagine that he was showing you that he

did not have to do as he was told, Maria. He is scarcely a boy in short coats any longer and it is only affection for us that impelled him to bring Lady Danby to us. You should not be so imperious in your dealings with him."

Lady Dora took a deep breath after her speech, amazed that her sister had allowed her to complete it. She was younger than Lady Granville, less aggressive, and she had never married. Despite these marked disadvantages, Lady Dora had never dwindled into a cipher as did many maiden ladies. Her nature was gentle, but her true strength lay in her deep and sincere affection for her family. Although she greatly disliked sharp words and unpleasant scenes, Lady Dora was fully capable of delivering a few home truths when necessary.

The dowager was aware of this and considered her sister's words thoughtfully. "Putting me in my place, is he? Perhaps. But what if he simply wanted no more of the widow's company?"

Lord Hartford, standing in the doorway, replied before his aunt could continue. "I assure you, Aunt, that I did not refuse because of Lady Danby."

"Alistair! Why did Ruffing not announce you? And who is that with you?"

Hartford gently propelled Lord Ashby toward his aunts. Looking most unhappy, Ashby bowed and murmured a few incoherent pleasantries. Hartford had torn him from his carriage just as he was departing for a congenial evening at White's and informed him that he was about to become an uninvited guest at a decidedly unpleasant family dinner. Horrified, Ashby had protested, but his companion had borne him inexorably to Grosvenor Square.

"Forgive me, Aunt. I assured Ruffing that there was no need to announce us and took the liberty of telling him to lay two more places for dinner."

Lady Granville looked at him sharply. "So that's it, is it, Alistair? You think that having Ashby at table with us will compel me to watch my tongue with the widow."

Alistair smiled at her and replied smoothly, "It merely occurred to me that our numbers were most uneven and that a gentleman of address such as Ashby would add to the pleasure of the evening. Besides which," he added, with a fine disregard for the truth that made Ashby blink, "I was already engaged to dine with Ashby and I had no desire to offend him."

"No offense taken, Hartford," replied his friend, a tall, loose-limbed young man. "No wish to intrude either. Not the thing at all." He bowed to the ladies. "You must be wishing me at Jericho. Told Hartford so, but he wouldn't listen." Ashby edged toward the door.

Lady Dora, who was in full agreement with her nephew that company was infinitely preferable to dining *en famille,* hurried to the unhappy Ashby before he could make good his escape. "Nonsense, Lord Ashby. We are delighted to have you. It has been this age since I have seen your good mother and I am eager to hear all about her." She placed her arm in his and led him relentlessly to the sofa.

At that moment Ruffing, perfectly expressionless, opened the door and announced, "Lady Sally Randolph and Sir Geoffrey Hayes."

"Hello, everyone," said Lady Sally breezily as she and Sir Geoffrey entered the room. Sir Geoffrey, a handsome, rather foppish young man, bowed to the assembled group as Lady Sally glanced at her brother. "I received your note, Alistair, and came straightaway. Where is Lady Danby?"

"She has not come down yet," said Alistair imperturbably, ignoring the dagger glance from Lady Granville. "I knew that you would wish to welcome her to London."

"Of course, Alistair," replied his sister impatiently. "Only I do hope that she is presentable, not some long Meg from the country or a poor little dab of a woman."

When Ruffing opened the door to the drawing room, it seemed to Violet that the room was filled with people, all of whom stopped talking and turned to stare at her as he announced her. She had, however, heard Lady Sally's remark most clearly, and she addressed herself to that fashionable young lady first.

"As you can see, I am by no means a long Meg, and although I am not tall, I have never heard myself described as a poor little dab of a woman either."

Lady Sally surveyed her approvingly. The dainty figure before her was arrayed in a high-waisted, celestial blue crepe, its short full sleeves slashed with white lace. Her dark hair was pulled back in a simple cluster of curls, a few light ringlets falling forward on each temple.

"How lovely you are," exclaimed Lady Sally, taking Violet's hand. "You must forgive my abominable tongue, Lady Danby. I am forever saying something that I do not mean. I am sure that we will deal extremely well together. Pray do not be cross with me."

Violet could not help smiling and replied, "Of course I am not cross, Lady Sally. It is most kind of you to take me in hand."

Lord Hartford took Violet's arm before his sister could continue and steered her across the room to his aunts. Lady Dora had already risen and embraced Violet warmly.

"We are so happy to have you come to us, my dear," she said, determined to have her word in before the dowager managed to say something offensive. "I have so longed to see dear Evan's wife. I am your Aunt Dora and this is your mama-in-law, Lady Granville."

Violet gave a small curtsey and hesitantly extended her hand to the dowager. She had not missed the uneasy note in kind Lady Dora's voice as she introduced her sister. Lady Granville nodded at her coolly, ignoring her outstretched hand. Violet flushed and let it fall to her side.

"I see that you are wearing the St. Clair brooch, Lady Danby," remarked the dowager in an arctic voice. Aunt Dora and Lord Hartford glanced at one another uneasily.

Violet's hand flew to the diamond brooch which was securely pinned in the white lace of her gown. She had not liked to wear it or the ring for fear of losing them, but she had decided that Penelope would expect it of her.

"Yes, Lady Granville. It is a lovely piece. Evan was very proud of it."

The dowager turned an alarming shade of purple and seemed unable to reply. Violet watched her uneasily, uncertain whether it was the mention of her dead son that had so distressed her. Lady Dora had produced the dowager's smelling salts and was quietly administering them when Ruffing announced that dinner was served.

The cook had risen grandly to the challenge of having four unexpected guests for dinner, and the assembled company partook comfortably of soup, removed with a loin of veal and partridges, accompanied by broiled mushrooms, buttered crab, French beans, and a Rhenish cream. The dowager, who recognized the fine hand of her nephew in all of this, was torn between amusement at his highhanded methods and irritation at being neatly outflanked. She decided to be amused and her relatives, relieved that she was not going to take a pet, relaxed and enjoyed themselves during dinner.

Violet, who had been carefully seated between Lady Dora and Lord Ashby, found herself feeling much more at ease than she had expected. Lady Dora sustained a comfortable flow of innocuous small talk, while Lord Ashby contributed his bit when there was an opportunity. The dowager was safely flanked by Lady Sally and Sir Geoffrey, and Lord Hartford, seated across the table from Violet, congratulated himself for rescuing her from what would have been a devilishly unpleasant dinner with Lady Granville.

A line creased his brow as he noticed again the brooch that she was wearing. It was a lovely little piece, fashioned like a butterfly with its wings spread

53

apart. It was quite unmistakable to anyone familiar with the St. Clair diamonds. His frown deepened as he saw that she was wearing the ring that belonged to the set as well. Both of these were traditionally worn by the reigning Countess of Granville, and Evan's widow would unfortunately antagonize the dowager still more by flaunting them. Lady Danby was either foolish beyond permission or she was deliberately courting disaster. The dowager still had not recovered from the fact that her only son had taken the family jewels from the secret drawer in her dressing table and sneaked away like a thief in the night. Lord Hartford found himself wondering what Evan had told his wife about those jewels.

When the ladies withdrew to leave the gentlemen with their port, Lady Sally directed a speaking look at her brother. Accordingly, poor Lord Ashby and Sir Geoffrey had scarcely taken a sip of their wine when Hartford announced that it was time to join the ladies.

Lady Sally tripped lightly into the drawing room beside Violet and whispered, "The gentlemen will join us soon. I expect that my aunt will try to eat us in the meantime. She is forever putting me in a quake by criticizing my dress or my behavior."

Violet smiled at her lively companion, grateful for her kindness. The dowager, who had taken note of the whispering, said, "What are you saying, Sally? Speak up so that we can hear you."

Lady Sally winked at Violet. "I was telling Lady Danby, Aunt, that it is of all things most fortunate that she is a brunette. We shall look amazingly well together." To emphasize her point, she struck a pose next to Violet, her golden hair sparkling in the light from the chandelier.

"Pretty pair of widgeons!" snorted Lady Granville unappreciatively.

"I do not believe that Lady Danby will need all of the help that you had anticipated, Aunt," said the irrepressible Sally. "My aunt was afraid that you would be an uncouth bumpkin, a complete antidote," she confided to Violet, "and that we would have to teach you manners and how to dress and go on in society."

"Indeed?" replied Violet coldly.

"No, no, don't poker up at me," pleaded Lady Sally. "Any clodpole could see that you are complete to a pin. I expect that you will be all the rage. I am, you know," she added complacently, "and we shall be always together."

"As you see, Lady Danby, my sister is a paragon of modesty," remarked Lord Hartford as he entered the room.

"Well, you know that it is true, Alistair," she pouted.

"Beyond a doubt, Lady Sally, you are a nonpareil," agreed Sir Geoffrey, bending over her attentively and kissing her hand. Lord Hartford watched this interchange with disapproval.

"Quite true, what Lady Sally said," commented Lord Ashby thoughtfully to his friend. "Expect that Lady Danby will be all the rage with the ton. Quite a taking little thing."

To his surprise, Lord Hartford found himself in agreement. He had not yet satisfied himself as to her character, but she was undeniably charming.

The small party broke up quite early that evening, Lady Dora announcing that she was certain that Lady Danby must be longing for her bed after her tiring journey. Violet gratefully escaped to her room without any further conversation with the dowager. Lady Sally and Sir Geoffrey departed for a soirée at Countess Lieven's home and Lords Hartford and Ashby retired gratefully to the gentlemanly joys of White's.

Before retiring to her bed, Violet carefully replaced Penelope's ring and brooch in their small velvet-lined case and put that away securely in a drawer of her dressing table. She had fully intended to thank Lady Granville for them, for Penelope had told her how Evan's mother had sent the two pieces to him secretly following his angry departure from Granville Court. Her gesture had given them hope of a reconciliation with his parents, but then Evan had been called back to duty. Soon afterwards had come the news of his death, and there had been nothing save cold silence from his parents. Still, Violet would have alluded to Lady Granville's one kindness in sending them had she not reacted in such an alarming manner to seeing the brooch. It must have reminded her too painfully of her son. Violet sighed. Undoubtedly the sight of it had brought back memories of Evan, and she clearly felt no kindness for his widow.

As she pulled the coverlets up to her chin, she wondered again how she had come to do such a caper-witted thing as impersonating Penelope. I must pluck up a little resolution, she told herself firmly. No one knows that I am not Lady Danby and I am hurting no one. I am in London and Lady Sally will take me everywhere with her. There will be no harm done and I may do a great deal of good if I can solve Penelope's problem. Comforted, she fell asleep.

Chapter Six

"I should think, Maria," said Lady Dora at breakfast the following morning, "that you would be delighted to find that Evan's widow is so charming. You were quite afraid that she would disgrace us."

"You are too easily gulled, Dora. We expected her to be well looking enough, and I grant you that she showed better taste in her dress than I had expected." She stirred her chocolate thoughtfully. "How do you suppose she is able to afford a modish gown like the one she wore last night? I thought she was quite penniless."

"I am certain there is a simple explanation, Maria," replied Lady Dora comfortably, helping herself to another slice of toast. She was fond of her creature comforts and intended to ignore Maria's restless probing while she enjoyed her breakfast.

"There is a simple explanation," said Violet, who had entered the dining room in time to hear their exchange. "If I had had no one to whom to turn, it is true that I would not have had a feather to fly with. But it is my good fortune to have an aunt who is most generous; there is nothing clutch-fisted about Aunt Serena."

"You are fortunate indeed," agreed Lady Granville frostily.

Violet, having by now taken the dowager's measure quite accurately, could not resist adding, "And my aunt was most fortunate to have married Mr. Philip Crawford. He was a quite successful sherry merchant and anything but a nip-farthing."

At the mention of Mr. Crawford's business connection, the dowager blanched and called for her smelling salts. "Trade!" she exclaimed weakly. "I might have expected it, but Evan assured me that your family was impoverished but perfectly respectable."

"Uncle Philip was perfectly respectable," returned Violet calmly, applying herself to the generous breakfast before her. "He simply decided that he preferred being plump in the pocket rather than impoverished."

The dowager cast her eyes heavenward, but found no counsel there.

"I am flattered, naturally, that you consider me well looking, Lady Granville," continued Violet, "but may I ask you in what way I gulled Lady Dora?"

Lady Dora looked longingly at the grilled kidneys still on her plate and then pushed it away. There would obviously be no peaceful breakfast today. She prepared to pour oil on the troubled waters.

"Maria is never at her best in the mornings," said Lady Dora soothingly. "There is no question of anyone being gulled, my dear, as we very well know."

The dowager's complexion darkened ominously, but before she could give Lady Dora the heavy set-down she so richly deserved, Lady Sally was announced and made her entrance, a vision in primrose muslin.

Both of her aunts were shocked into speechlessness by her unexpected appearance. At this hour of the day Lady Sally was usually still in her bed amid a sea of lacy pillows, drinking her morning chocolate and perusing the gilt-edged invitations that had arrived in the early mail.

"I have come to take you to Madame Celeste," she announced to Violet. "You will be needing new gowns, you know, for there will be so many parties to attend, and you will not be wanting to wear the same thing to them."

Violet could not have agreed with her more. She hurried upstairs to change her dress, grateful to Lady Sally for offering her a means of escape from the dowager's clutches. With Summers' help, she quickly slipped into a round dress of jaconet muslin and a spencer of dark blue *gros de Naples* richly ornamented with white satin. Her bonnet was composed of white satin, the edge of the brim finished by rouleaux of blue and white plaid silk, and a large bow of the same material and a plume of ostrich feathers perched jauntily on one side of the crown. White gloves and trim little half boots completed her ensemble.

"Now, miss," said Summers with satisfaction, "you look as fine as any of the fashionable London ladies you will see today."

Secure in the knowledge that she looked precise to a pin, Violet tripped downstairs to join Lady Sally, and together they set off, both of them prepared to be ogled by the Bond Street beaux.

It was an entirely blissful day for Violet. She recklessly ordered morning gowns, walking dresses, a smart riding habit, evening dresses, and the three new ball gowns that Lady Sally assured her were the minimum needed. Together they compared the merits of an extremely dashing promenade dress of amber creped muslin with those of an enchanting Dresden blue walking dress. Finding themselves in agreement on every point as they settled on the creped muslin, they congratulated one another on their mutual good taste and returned to Lady Sally's carriage quite in charity with one another.

From Leicester Square they went next to the establishment of *plumassier* W.H. Botibol in Oxford Street to examine his supply of "Ostrich and Fancy Feathers and Artificial Flowers." Having decided that her spending had been quite prodigal that morning, Lady Sally had decided to economize by refurbishing one of her straw bonnets herself. Finally, after discarding dozens of plumes as too dear or too stringy, abusing a bunch of artificial cherries as ugly beyond belief, and rejecting a wreath of moss roses on the grounds that it did not become her, Lady Sally abandoned her praiseworthy objective, and, leaving the clerk who had attended them limp with relief, they retired once more to her stylish barouche.

"Well, at least we did not spend any more," remarked Lady Sally virtuously. "I am quite certain that I have used up all of my quarter's allowance today, and I shan't even receive it until next week."

Violet listened to her friend's careless remarks with some discomfort. She was not precisely sure how much she had actually spent that morning herself, for Madame Celeste would not have dreamed of mentioning money to the daughter-in-law of the Dowager Countess of Granville. Too, Lady Sally Randolph was one of her most valued clients, for Lord Randolph, unlike many of the nobility, paid his bills promptly and saw to it that his wife did also, and Lady Sally also displayed the modiste's creations to remarkable advantage. Violet had allowed herself to be directed by her friend, so surely all would work out well. She comforted herself with the thought that Aunt Serena had given her a substantial amount of money and promptly put the matter from her mind.

Exhausted by their exertions, the two young ladies repaired to Berkley Square to refresh themselves with ices from Gunter's. The coachman found a shady place under the plane trees for their barouche, and a waiter from the famous confectioner's came dashing across the road to wait on them. Two gentlemen who had been lazily lounging against the railings disengaged themselves from their group and made their way toward Lady Sally and Violet.

Lady Sally saw them coming and her face brightened. "Geoffrey!" she called happily, extending her hand. "I had hoped to see you here. You remember Sir Geoffrey Hayes, do you not, Violet?"

Violet nodded and smiled at the handsome young man. His companion, a considerably older man with a somewhat saturnine expression, bowed to the ladies.

"Allow me to present Sir Reginald Hawke," said Sir Geoffrey. "Sir Reginald, Lady Sally Randolph and Lady Danby."

"I am honored, ladies." He bowed courteously, taking each of their hands in turn. He held Violet's hand a little too long and she moved uncomfortably under his bold gaze.

Lady Sally was oblivious to this interchange, for she was deep in conversation with Sir Geoffrey. At her invitation, the two gentlemen joined them in the barouche, and Violet found herself obliged to converse with Sir Reginald.

"I understand that you have not been in London long," he commented easily.

"No, I arrived only yesterday, sir," Violet replied.

"I was certain that you could have been here no longer than that."

"Why is that, Sir Reginald?" she asked, uneasy lest she had done something to show herself a provincial.

"Such a charming face as yours could not have escaped my notice had you been here longer." His words were innocent enough, but his gaze was intense, and Violet felt herself coloring.

"Altogether charming," he commented, claiming her hand and kissing it before she could draw it away.

To her relief, Lady Sally suddenly turned to her with a glowing face. "You shall never guess, Violet. It is the most famous thing imaginable!"

Violet, anxious to be saved from her tête-à-tête, professed herself eager to know her friend's news.

"Geoffrey wishes to take us to see Eliza Vestris in *The Beggar's Opera* tonight. She plays the part of Macheath and everyone talks of her, you know. Do say that you will go!"

Violet was most happy to lend her support to this scheme, although her pleasure was somewhat diminished when she found that Sir Reginald was to accompany them.

"Is it quite all right?" she asked Lady Sally after the gentlemen had taken their leave. "I mean, is it all right for us to go to the theatre with only two gentleman to accompany us?"

Lady Sally looked offended. "I should hardly recommend that we go if it were not the thing to do," she retorted. "After all, I am a married lady and you are a widow. We shall be perfectly respectable."

"I did not mean to criticize," said Violet apologetically. "Perhaps when I have been here longer I shall know better how to go on."

Lady Sally's frown disappeared. "Of course you cannot be expected to know when you've only just come to London. I am the one who should beg your pardon. I promise that I will stop pinching at you if you stop looking so Friday-faced. A fine pair we make!" And the awkward moment disappeared and was forgotten, Violet resolving to trust her new friend implicitly.

Her first evening at Covent Garden was not a time of unalloyed pleasure. As she had feared, the dowager was out of sorts because she was attending the theatre with Lady Sally and only two gentlemen, and even Lady Dora seemed doubtful. Fortunately, however, Lady Granville recalled that she herself was responsible for Violet being in Lady Sally's company and promptly put an end to her sister's lingering doubts.

The play itself was delightful, and Violet, leaning forward in her chair so that she would miss nothing, was enchanted by Eliza Vestris. During the intervals, however, she was less happily occupied. Sir Geoffrey claimed all of Lady Sally's attention, and Violet was left to suffer Sir Reginald's fulsome compliments.

She was relieved when Lord Hartford and his friend Ashby joined them in their box during the second interval, although Lady Sally did not seem particularly pleased to see them.

Hartford bowed stiffly to the gentlemen and addressed himself to Violet. "I trust that you are enjoying the performance, Lady Danby."

"Indeed I am," she replied, her eyes shining. "Miss Vestris is wonderful . . . so very talented."

He drew his chair closer to her. "Had I known you wished to see her, I would have invited you myself. I called at Granville House this afternoon to place myself at your command for the evening."

"How kind of you," she replied, with some surprise and more than a little regret. She would have infinitely preferred to attend the play in his company rather than Sir Reginald's. "Your sister was kind enough to take me shopping with her today," she explained.

"So I understand," he replied in amusement. "I hope that she did not encourage you to spend a king's ransom as she does."

Lady Sally, overhearing him, remarked indignantly, "How odiously unjust, Alistair! I only helped Violet select the absolutely essential things she will need. Nothing more!"

Her brother held up his hands in mock terror. "I cry pardon! I had forgotten how sober you have become now that you are a matron."

He arose from his chair, and he and his friend made

their way back to their own seats. With a small frown, he noticed that Sir Reginald once again moved his chair close to Violet and that Sir Geoffrey's dark head bent far too close to Sally's golden curls. His troublesome sister was too rackety by half, and the company of the lovely widow was not likely to do anything to improve the tone of her mind. Lady Danby's first night in London and she chose to spend it with a notorious rake like Sir Reginald Hawke.

Chapter Seven

Lady Sally looked enchanting in a demure morning gown of sprigged lilac muslin, but the lovely picture she presented was lost upon her brother, who proceeded to enlighten her about his feelings regarding her conduct with Sir Geoffrey Hayes in a few pithy sentences.

"You forget, Alistair, that I am a married woman," she said haughtily, trying desperately for an air of dignity. "It is my husband that I must answer to for my conduct, not my brother."

"Gammon!" replied Lord Hartford brutally. "Your husband is two thousand miles away and it is as well for you that he is. Were he any closer you might be certain that some scandal-monger would have already informed him that his young wife is fast becoming one of the *on-dits* of the ton."

Lady Sally's chin quivered dangerously. "How can you say that, Alistair, when you know that I have done nothing so terribly wrong?"

He relented slightly. "Not as yet perhaps," he conceded, "but you are allowing Hayes to be far too particular in his attentions. You may have admirers, yes; Randolph would certainly not expect you to sit at home. But you may *not* attach one gentleman only, Sally; no newly married female is allowed such license. Randolph is a patient man, but not that patient."

She dabbed at her eyes pathetically. "But I do get lonely, Alistair, and Sir Geoffrey has been so kind."

"Much *too* kind," he replied grimly. "I shall soon put an end to that."

"Alistair, no!" she shrieked. "You would not disgrace me so! I forbid you to mention this matter to Geoffrey!"

"Understand me, Sally. I will honor your wishes in this matter only if you will promise me to put an end to it."

"Put an end to it? May I not even see him in company?" she asked, horrified.

"Certainly you may . . . but in company. No more of the private little parties like the one Ash and I interrupted last night." He put his finger beneath her chin and forced her to look at him. "Have I your word?"

"Oh, yes, I suppose so," she said sulkily. "I suppose that you must have your way and run roughshod over the rest of us."

"Poor Sally," he said laughingly, "you will find something else to amuse you. Give your energies to introducing Lady Danby into society. That will keep you safely occupied."

"Well, of all the unreasonable—," she gasped. "Pray, what did you think I was doing last night?"

"Don't try to bamboozle me, my girl. Last night you were flirting madly with Hayes and you had abandoned Lady Danby to a curst rum touch."

"Sir Reginald?" she asked, wide-eyed. "But he is received everywhere and he seemed quite taken with Penelope."

"I daresay," Hartford replied drily, "but Lady Danby is not up to snuff and Hawke is a dashed loose screw. How did she come to be with him?"

Lady Sally, unwilling to admit her assignation with Sir Geoffrey at Gunter's, replied airily, "He saw us at Gunter's yesterday and introduced himself to Penelope. I already knew him, of course. When he invited her to the theatre and she so wanted to go, I told her I must go to play propriety."

"And I suppose that Hayes just happened to be available as your escort?" She nodded.

He looked at her in exasperation. "How our aunt came up with the jingle-brained notion of making you responsible for Lady Danby, I cannot imagine."

"Aunt Maria knew that I would see that she is invited to all of the ton parties, of course," she answered impatiently.

"Then I suggest that you do so," he recommended, "without the help of Sir Geoffrey or Sir Reginald. And remember that you have given me your word."

Lady Sally nodded, still pouting, and Lord Hartford took his leave, telling her that he must drive to Hartford Park, but that he would return in time to escort her and Lady Danby to Lady Halliburton's ball. He was grateful for the business affairs that called him away from London just now, for he was beginning to take too great an interest in Lady Danby.

Lady Sally was as good as her word, and for the next three days she and Violet paid countless calls upon ladies of the ton, went riding in the Park at five each afternoon, attended two rout parties, an al fresco breakfast, and a waltzing party. Dazzled but delighted, Violet found herself very favorably received. Her beauty and good nature, combined with her stylish appearance, good family, and Lady Sally's patronage, assured her success with the ton and made her the envy of many another less fortunate young woman. She had also the distinction of being the widow of one of the heroes of Salamanca, which gave her an added aura of romance.

Lady Sally managed to convey a tactful warning to Sir Geoffrey and he in turn apparently shared it with Sir Reginald, for Violet saw little of either gentleman for several days, and she was relieved to be free of the older man's disturbing presence. She quite enjoyed herself flirting with the young smarts she met at the parties, for they could be trusted to keep the line. It was not at all the same as finding oneself in a box with a gentleman forcing his attentions upon one. Indeed, she soon found herself with a faithful following of her own.

When Lord Hartford escorted them to Lady Halliburton's ball on the following Thursday evening, he was amused to see the disparity in the level of anticipation with which each lady awaited the evening. Violet leaned forward eagerly, watching everything from the carriage window, while Sally leaned languidly against the cushions. This would be Violet's first London ball, and she was carefully arrayed in a three-quarter dress of white spider gauze worn over a slip of coral satin; Sally was once again a vision in gold, her gauze gown tinted the same guinea gold as her hair.

Violet enjoyed herself beyond measure that evening.

She never wanted for partners and received them all, whether old or young, single or married, with a charming smile. Her enthusiasm and graceful ways endeared her, causing Lady Sally to observe tartly to her brother that one would think Violet was setting her cap for every man with which she danced.

"Sour grapes, Sally?" he inquired teasingly.

She tossed her head. "I wish you will not be funning me, Alistair. I am not so lost to all sense of propriety as to throw myself at the head of every available man!"

"No," he agreed gravely. "As I recall, you were satisfied with simply throwing yourself at one gentleman's head."

"Alistair! Of all the odious—"

"That was unhandsome of me, wasn't it, Sally?" he replied ruefully. "I do beg your pardon."

Their conversation was interrupted by the arrival of Lord Ashby, who, having heard the last portion of their interchange and seeing Sally's angry flush, asked knowingly, "A little cross-and-jostle work?"

Lady Sally, having known Lord Ashby from the cradle, replied frostily, "I wish that you would strive for a little more conduct, Ashby!"

"Having a fit of the dismals, is she?" he asked of Hartford as Lady Sally stalked away.

"She is not accustomed to playing second fiddle," replied his friend, watching as Sir Reginald Hawke led Violet out to dance.

Following his glance, Ashby commented, "That's a dashed fine girl, Alistair. Young. To see her, you'd never guess that she was a widow."

"No," said Hartford drily. "You would not. She disguises it remarkably well."

"Won't stay one long. A widow, I mean. Mark my words." Pleased with his omniscient observation, Ashby repaired to the card room, leaving his friend black-browed and thoughtful.

Violet was surprised and not particularly pleased that Lord Hartford had put his name down for a dance. When he finally came to claim his waltz, she was prepared with a bright smile and a host of trivial comments that he scarcely acknowledged, caught as he was between his admiration of her liveliness of spirit and his conviction that such behavior was not entirely suitable for a widow. When the last of these had been exhausted, an uneasy silence settled over them that Violet was determined not to break.

When the music ended, Hartford led her back to her place, but before taking his leave as she had expected, he took her hand in his and addressed her intently.

"Lady Danby, would you accompany me on a drive round the Park tomorrow afternoon?"

Violet told herself that she had no desire to go, but she could think of no suitable excuse that would not be insulting, and so she consented. She thought it was amazing that he would burden himself with the company of someone that he so obviously held in contempt and wondered if perhaps she was to receive a lecture for some misdoing. That seemed the likeliest solution to the question, and, although she did not anticipate enduring a scold with any particular pleasure, she cared too little for his good opinion to be distressed.

The day after the ball passed agreeably enough for Violet. She slept late and then entertained a succession of morning callers, who had come to inspect and admire the new belle. That afternoon she had promised Lady Sally to attend a small card party with her at the home of one of her friends, a Mrs. Ellen Mason.

"I really only know her to bow to," Lady Sally confided during their drive to Mrs. Mason's, "but Geoffrey says that her parties are very select and quite unexceptionable."

"Sir Geoffrey?" asked Violet doubtfully. "I had not thought that you were seeing him any more."

"Alistair told me that I could not have Geoffrey living in my pocket," she said airily, "and indeed I have not. I am certain that Alistair would not wish for me to cut his acquaintance altogether."

Violet, who felt some doubts about the likelihood of Lord Hartford agreeing with her optimistic view, wisely held her peace.

They found that Mrs. Mason's party was small and very tasteful. Card tables were scattered throughout the double drawing room and a table of refreshments was provided in the dining room. Lady Sally and Violet recognized a few of the ladies as nodding acquaintances, but most of them, although very elegant in appearance, were unknown to them. There were no more than three or four gentlemen, who moved quietly through the rooms, stopping to converse at the various tables.

Violet settled happily at a table with Lady Sally, Mrs. Mason, and a quiet young woman named Miss Gibbings, who devoted all of her attention to the cards. Violet and Mrs. Crawford had spent many a winter evening playing at piquet and she quite looked forward to playing a rubber or two. Her eyes widened a little when she realized that they would be playing for money and her startled glance flew to Lady Sally, who nonchalantly suggested that they play for shilling points.

Violet played her cards intently, for she had no intention of losing any of her precious money. She was an experienced player and her understanding was good, but it was soon obvious that Mrs. Mason and Miss Gibbings were not to be despised. Lady Sally, careless of her cards, spent much of her time observing what was taking place at the other tables and relating it to the three seated with her.

At one point, her eyebrows rose and she exclaimed softly, "Lady Shelton has just wagered her pearl necklace." Across the room Violet could see a thin woman wearing a purple turban quietly unfasten a rope of pearls and place it on the table before her. Mrs. Mason and Miss Gibbings seemed to see nothing out of the way in this and continued their playing unperturbed.

"I daresay she will win it back directly," remarked Mrs. Mason without emotion. "She usually does. Sometimes she stakes her diamond bracelet, but she prefers to use the pearls."

At the end of two rubbers, Violet was pleased to find herself with a very comfortable sum to add to the money she carried in her reticule. Lady Sally, however, had lost quite heavily and discovered that she had not enough with her to pay her debt. Violet immediately offered to loan her the amount, but Mrs. Mason exclaimed against this.

"Your vowel is quite good enough, dear Lady Sally." Sally, relieved to have the matter taken care of so easily, scribbled her signature on the slip of paper Mrs. Mason offered her.

"I quite enjoyed that, did not you, Penelope?" she inquired on the drive back to Granville House. "I daresay that I may win the next time we attend."

Violet did not reply; honesty forbade her to agree with Sally's characteristically optimistic view of the situation. Her thoughtless bidding had indicated little aptitude for the game, and on her account Violet had been relieved that they had stayed no longer.

"Of course, I shall send round the money I owe to Mrs. Mason tomorrow morning. I know that discharging one's gaming debts promptly is a point of honor." She giggled suddenly. "Just imagine Alistair's face if he knew that I had a gaming debt, even a tiny one like this."

Violet, who had no difficulty at all picturing Lord Hartford's expression when he was displeased, asked hesitantly, "Is it so very bad then to have a debt such as yours?"

Lady Sally waved her hand lightly. "Of course it is not. Gentlemen, including my starched-up brother, think nothing of playing deep themselves, and any number of ladies of the nobility do the same. But Alistair would keep me wrapped in cotton wool and not allow me the tiniest morsel of fun if he could manage it. Such Gothic notions!"

She paused for a moment, then added idly, with a nonchalance that did not for a moment deceive her companion, "I had thought to see Sir Geoffrey there. He had mentioned that he looks in quite frequently."

Violet understood then the attraction of Mrs. Mason's card party. Lady Sally had been hopeful of seeing Sir Geoffrey in a situation that could in no way be described as a tête-à-tête. She felt some sympathy for that enterprising young lady, for she could identify with Sally's boredom. Just so had she felt when she had made the outrageous decision to impersonate Penelope. Her own behavior struck her as much more outré than that of Sally, who merely wished to conduct an innocent flirtation with a handsome young man.

At five o'clock precisely, Lord Hartford called for Violet, dressed in leather breeches and top-boots, a well-fitting drab driving coat over all.

"Are you quite ready, ma'am?" he asked, sounding somewhat impatient.

Violet nodded briskly, pulling on her straw-colored gloves as Ruffing opened the door for them. Hartford's groom was awaiting them, holding a spirited, handsome pair of grays.

"What fine-looking animals," she exclaimed as he helped her into the curricle.

"They are, aren't they?" he agreed, springing up beside her and nodding to his groom. "I won't be needing you, Kendall," he said. "You may wait for me here."

Together they bowled smoothly out of the square and into Upper Grosvenor Street. Violet silently admired his handling of the ribbons and wondered more than ever what could have induced this proud, silent man to take her driving.

The answer was not long in coming. As they entered the Park, nodding now and then to friends that they passed, Hartford reached into the pocket of his driving coat and drew out a lovely silver snuffbox, ornately engraved, and handed it to her.

"When I was at Hartford Park, I came across this, Lady Danby, and thought that you might like to have it."

76

Violet looked at him with a puzzled expression and he explained. "It belonged to Evan. He must have left it when he was visiting the Park — years ago, of course. He had quite a collection of snuffboxes, and so he wouldn't have missed one. You know how fond of snuff he was."

Violet, who had scarcely known her late brother-in-law at all, knew no such thing, but she smiled at Lord Hartford and after admiring it properly, tucked the box away in her reticule.

"That was most kind of you, Lord Hartford."

Hartford bowed and a brief, uncomfortable silence ensued.

"It does not distress you, then, seeing something that belonged to your late husband?"

Violet replied hesitantly, feeling like a traitor to Penelope. "No, it does not upset me, precisely. It all seems so long ago, you see, almost as though it happened to someone else." That much at least was true she thought with satisfaction.

"That is what I thought it must be," he said eagerly. "You and Evan were little more than children when you married."

Violet remained silent, wondering at his eagerness, and in a moment he continued.

"It is because of that circumstance that I feel free to speak to you, Lady Danby. I will not conceal from you that I feel some misgivings about the suitability of such a match. Your unfortunate marriage, your youth and lack of judgment — all of these are reasons for me to doubt the wisdom of making such a choice, but the strength of my emotion has quite overcome my fears. I must ask you, Lady Danby, if you will marry me."

Had he announced that she was about to become the Queen of Spain, Violet could not have been more astounded. Nothing—no word, or look, or gesture—had prepared her for his declaration. She sat in silence for a moment, trying to gather her scattered thoughts.

"I am afraid, Lord Hartford, that you have cast me into some confusion. I had not expected such a declaration."

"I regret my abruptness, Lady Danby, but the degree of awkwardness that I felt prohibited my speaking with greater address. Forgive me."

"There is nothing to forgive, Lord Hartford. I am sensible of the fact that you believe you have done me a great honor in asking for my hand." She paused, searching for words. It was impossible to consider marrying this haughty, proper man who would forever be finding fault with her family and her behavior! But how astonishing that he had overcome his distaste for her background and her failings enough to speak of marriage. His feelings must be strong indeed. For a moment her chin quivered as she pictured the disgust that he would inevitably feel when he knew of her charade.

Seeing her distress, he spoke quickly. "I have upset you. I am most truly sorry, Lady Danby."

She shook her head. "No, you have not, Lord Hartford." She stared down at her tightly clasped hands. "Indeed I appreciate the honor you have done me, but I fear that I cannot accept." She took courage and looked at him directly. "You were right, sir. We should not suit, you know."

"I see," he answered briefly. "I must appreciate the candor of your response."

The ride back to Granville House was a silent one. He helped her from the curricle and escorted her to the door.

"May I offer you a piece of advice in parting, Lady Danby?" She nodded, wondering what he might say.

"I say this because I know you are not familiar with town life, madam. I would suggest that you not encourage the attentions of a man such as Sir Reginald Hawke. He is highly ineligible and it would be best for you if you cut the connection altogether."

Violet flushed angrily. She had no desire to encourage Sir Reginald, but it rankled to have Lord Hartford taking it upon himself to tell her what to do. Still more did it rankle that he obviously believed that she *had* encouraged Sir Reginald.

"I appreciate your well-meant advice, sir, but I fancy that I can judge such matters for myself," she returned sharply.

There was a moment of uneasy silence as he looked down at her.

"Your servant, ma'am," he said briefly, bowing to her as Ruffing opened the door.

Violet sat before her dressing table long that night and stared pensively at her reflection. She had received her first proposal, and from a peer of the realm, but she felt curiously deflated. She knew that her response had been the only one possible. He was an overbearing, insufferably proud man and he would always have found her lacking. She shuddered, thinking of the distaste that he would feel when he knew the truth about her masquerade. He would be grateful then for her refusal.

She would have been angry indeed had she known

that Lord Hartford was already grateful for her refusal. Common sense told him that such a marriage would never do. Not only would he be marrying beneath his station, but he also would be taking a wife whose character seemed strangely contradictory and out of keeping with his own. Fortunate indeed that she had realized better than he that they would not suit.

Chapter Eight

To her relief, Violet was not called upon to face Lord Hartford for some time after his declaration in the Park. Lady Sally told her carelessly the following day that he had once again been called away on business.

"At least I need not live in fear of receiving another of his scolds for the time being," she remarked happily. "He was quite brutal about poor Sir Geoffrey, and so needlessly, too. It is quite dreadfully uncomfortable to feel that one may be pounced on at any time for some imaginary wrongdoing."

Violet, her conscience weighing heavily upon her, agreed that this was a most uncomfortable feeling indeed. She felt no desire to tell Lady Sally of her brother's declaration; indeed, she was sometimes inclined to believe that she had imagined it all. Anxious to put the matter from her mind, she was happy to join her friend in an even gayer whirl of ton parties, hoping that constant activity would help to assuage her growing feeling of guilt.

Although the dowager was as brusque and peremptory in manner as ever, at Lady Dora's insistence she had given a dinner in Violet's honor and had even gone so far as to make her an allowance. Violet had attempted to refuse the allowance, but the dowager had brushed her protests aside impatiently. "I know what is due to my son's wife, even if Dora thinks I don't," she had said sharply. Violet found Lady Granville's manner difficult to decipher, for an apparently kindly gesture such as this might well be followed by a particularly offensive remark or a curiously oblique reference to the St. Clair diamonds which she found particularly unsettling. There seemed to be an extraordinary interest in her jewelry, she had noticed. Even Sally had been interested in her ring and brooch, inquiring as to whether or not she possessed other diamonds.

Lady Dora was quite another matter, however, thought Violet affectionately. She had done her utmost to make Evan's widow feel at home and it was her kindness that made Violet feel most wretched about her deception. If Penelope's reception at Granville House had rested solely with Lady Dora, Violet would have felt no hesitation in confessing everything to her. Unfortunately, however, the dowager was much less approachable, and Penelope and Evan's well-being would rest with her. She devoted little thought to the absent Lord Granville and what his feelings might be if he knew that his title was not rightfully his.

The golden days of September slipped into October and still Lord Hartford and Lord Granville stayed busy at their respective estates. Penelope and Mrs. Crawford wrote often, urging her to come home to them soon, but Violet put them off, floating through her days in a delightful haze, promising herself that soon she would think of a way to win back Evan's inheritance. To go back to Stanhope Cottage was to return to her old solitary way of life and she could not yet face it. Penelope reproached her sister for forgetting them, and told her that she would not be able to rest easily again until Violet was safely home. Violet felt guilty, knowing that Penny feared for her son, but she tucked that letter away with the others in the drawer of the dressing table, assuring herself that soon she would indeed go home. She quieted her conscience by sending Penelope the silver snuffbox that Lord Hartford had given her, although she did not tell her of his proposal, still feeling oddly hesitant to mention it to anyone.

Her days were filled now with the whirl of gaiety that she had dreamed of during her quiet days at Stanhope Cottage. There was no lady of the ton who was livelier or more entertaining or more sought after than the vivacious, vivid Lady Danby. The dowager and Lady Dora received a seemingly endless parade of callers at Granville House and found that their mail had tripled in bulk since Violet's arrival.

"What does the chit mean by causing all this hubble-bubble of activity?" demanded Lady Granville of her sister. "Don't she realize that she is a widow and her activities should be more seemly?"

"Well, she is very young," temporized Lady Dora, "and she cannot help being so pretty. Aside from which," she added candidly, "she goes everywhere with Sally, and you know that is just what you told her to do."

"I did not know that she would make a spectacle of herself!"

"I don't know that she is doing so," remarked her sister, pondering the matter thoughtfully. "Her disposition is lively and playful and it is to be expected that people, gentlemen especially, would find her very refreshing."

"Bah!" The dowager thumped her cane against the floor. "Did you know that they are calling her the Merry Widow?" she demanded furiously.

"No, I had not heard that." Lady Dora paused and remarked gently, "Quite apt, is it not?" thereby reducing her sister to speechless fury.

Violet and Lady Sally had fallen into the habit of attending Mrs. Mason's card parties several times a week, and Violet found that she quite looked forward to them, particularly as she usually won. Lady Sally unfortunately lost more often than not, but occasionally Sir Geoffrey was in attendance and her game usually improved with him to guide her. Violet was uneasily aware that Lady Sally had been obliged to offer Mrs. Mason her vowel upon several occasions, always refusing Violet's offer of a loan. Which was just as well, Violet reflected, for her own supply of ready cash had dwindled amazingly. Despite Mrs. Crawford's original gift of money and the dowager's allowance, Violet found that living in London was shockingly expensive. One could not be always wearing the same gowns, and there were so many affairs to attend. She had steadfastly refused to accept any more money from her aunt, knowing that Mrs. Crawford did not really approve of her remaining in London. In view of her pressing circumstances, Violet deemed it most fortunate indeed that she was an astute card player, and grew to rely upon the small sums that she won regularly at Mrs. Mason's.

After a particularly costly run of bad luck one afternoon, Lady Sally horrified Violet by unfastening a lovely little diamond bracelet from her wrist and placing it on the table.

"Perhaps this will bring me luck," she said recklessly.

"Sally, do not stake your bracelet. You must not," said Violet in a low voice, remembering that the bracelet had been a gift from her husband.

"It is of no consequence," she replied breezily. "I do feel that my luck is in this time."

Unfortunately, Lady Sally played quite as poorly in that rubber as she had in the earlier ones, and she and Violet watched in stunned silence as a newcomer to the game, a gentleman with a smiling manner named Captain Andrews, dropped the bracelet into his waistcoat pocket.

"I hate to win from a lady," he said with an apologetic air. "I am sure that we can arrange for you to have your bauble back again, my dear."

Lady Sally decided to overlook his familiarity in her relief. "I shall certainly redeem it from you, sir, if you will but tell me your direction. I will send one of my footmen to you."

In the privacy of her carriage, Lady Sally allowed herself the privilege of bursting into tears.

"How came we to be playing for so much money, Penelope?" she asked pitifully.

In truth, Violet herself had not noticed how the stakes had crept up with every game they played.

There had been no real problem until now.

"At least Captain Andrews appears to be a gentleman," she said consolingly. "But, Sally, how will you redeem the bracelet? I thought that you had no more pin money until the next quarter day."

"I haven't," said Sally despairingly, "but I will think of a way. I must! John would never understand."

"I do not have that much," replied Violet slowly, "but I would like to help you."

"You are so very good," said Sally, squeezing her arm affectionately. She closed her eyes for a moment. "I am so grateful that Alistair is not in London. He would be quite livid if he were to find out."

Violet shuddered in silent agreement and puzzled quietly over a possible solution. When the carriage arrived at Granville House, they had not yet decided upon their course of action, and Sally clutched her friend's hand.

"Promise me, Penelope, that you will come to me tomorrow morning."

"Of course I will," answered Violet briskly, sounding a great deal more confident than she felt. "Everything will be quite all right."

The morning came, but brought with it no fresh inspiration; indeed, when Violet arrived at Lady Sally's home on Hill Street, she saw from her friend's face that it had brought disaster instead.

"What is it? What has happened, Sally?" asked Violet as soon as the door to the small morning room closed behind the butler.

"It is too awful for words, Penelope. I am undone. Alistair will see to it that my husband sends me away to the country until he comes home again to England."

"Why? Whatever has happened?"

It was some minutes before Violet could extract a coherent account from her friend. It seemed that Captain Andrews was not such a gentleman after all, and he had suggested in a note to Sally that if she were unable to redeem the bracelet herself, her brother, the illustrious Marquess of Hartford, might be interested in doing so.

"Alistair will do more than ring a peal over me if he comes to know of this!" wailed Sally. "He will do something quite dreadful! I know that he will!"

Violet felt that Sally was undoubtedly correct in her fears, but she tried to be comforting. "Do not be in such a taking, Sally. Let us think of what we might do. After all, your brother is not in London now and so Captain Andrews will have to wait until he returns to approach him."

Sally's expression clearly revealed that Violet had offered her but cold comfort. "That is the worst of it, Penelope. Just when Alistair should stay at Hartford Park, what must he need do but come back again to London." She waved a crumpled sheet of stationery at her friend. "I had his letter in the morning post. He will be back in time to escort me to Lady Rothmore's party tomorrow night!"

They sat in silence for a few moments, quite sunk by the trouble that had come upon them.

Suddenly Violet sat bolt upright in her chair. "Sally! What a goose I have been! I am quite out of patience with myself!"

Lady Sally's face brightened magically. "Have you

thought of something then?"

"I have, slow-top though I have been." She turned to her friend. "You have lost a great deal of money playing piquet at Mrs. Mason's, have you not?"

Lady Sally nodded her agreement to this painfully obvious statement.

Violet looked at her complacently. "And what of me, Sally? Have I lost money as well?"

"Very little," replied Lady Sally. "In fact, you have won quite steadily. So might I have if my cards had been better," she added somewhat petulantly.

"You would not have played them well if you had had them," said Violet brutally. "The great point is that I have won almost every rubber I have played. I shall play this afternoon again, but this time I shall play for higher stakes than I have before.

Comprehension began to dawn in Lady Sally's eyes. "Penelope! How famous! You will win enough money so that I can get the bracelet back before Alistair arrives in town!" She sprang to her feet and threw her arms around her friend. "How shall I ever be able to thank you?"

"I will be happy to do it. I think it is quite underhanded of Captain Andrews to behave in such a paltry way. He must be completely lacking in honor."

That afternoon Violet went to Mrs. Mason's alone, carrying with her in her reticule every farthing that she and Sally could scrape together. With great determination, she seated herself at a table whose players were known for the high stakes they considered necessary for proper enjoyment of the game. To her consternation, she saw that Sir Reginald was also seated there, but she could not allow that to sway her. As the game progressed, it became clear to the others that she was extremely intent upon her game, much more single-minded than she had been on other days.

"I see that Lady Sally did not accompany you today," remarked an older woman at the table.

"She had another engagement," said Violet briefly.

"It was a shame about her bracelet," remarked the lady idly. "Such a pretty one, too."

Sir Reginald's eyebrows shot up. "What is this?" he inquired curiously. "Lady Sally must have gotten badly dipped to give up her jewelry."

"Not at all," replied Violet sharply. "It was just a stupid misunderstanding. She shall soon have it back again."

"Shall she indeed?" he asked, looking at her thoughtfully. She flushed under his scrutiny and turned her attention again to the cards.

As the afternoon wore on, Violet realized that she was playing with more seasoned gamesters than she had dealt with before and she saw with horror that she was beginning to lose quite heavily. She had quite used up her modest supply of money, and she knew that she could not give her vowel, for she could expect no more money for several weeks. Even if she appealed to her aunt, the money would not arrive for several days, and Violet could not bear to think how Aunt Serena would feel if she were petitioned for money to pay for Violet's gambling debts. If only she had enough money to play in the next rubber, she must surely win! Her luck could not be out all afternoon long.

As she considered her options, Violet looked up to

see Sir Reginald studying her, a smile playing about his lips.

"Perhaps, Lady Danby, you would like to do as Lady Sally did and stake a piece of your jewelry? Perhaps that dainty brooch you wear so often?"

Violet's hand flew to the brooch and she opened her mouth to refuse, but the words died on her lips. She would surely win if she played again. For a moment Penelope's face rose reproachfully before her, but then she thought of Sally's dilemma, and she made up her mind. Quickly she unfastened the pin and placed it on the table.

It was quite dark when the carriage set Violet down again in Hill Street and Lady Sally drew her eagerly into the drawing room.

"Well? Did you manage it, Penelope? Have we enough money to send to Captain Andrews?"

Violet stared at her, her face expressionless. "Not only have we not got enough money for that, Sally, nor indeed any money at all, but I have also lost my diamond brooch to Sir Reginald."

There was a silence and then Lady Sally flew to her feet and paced restlessly back and forth down the length of the room. Had Violet expected her friend to offer any consolation, she would have been sadly disappointed. Like many another, Lady Sally was too overcome by her own misfortune to think of the plight of another.

"Alistair will soon know," she murmured, wiping her eyes.

Violet rose to take her leave. "I am sorry, Sally," she said quietly, but her companion did not hear her, and continued her unhappy pacing.

Long after the rest of the household was asleep that night, Violet lay in her room and stared at the ceiling. What she had done had been thoughtless, without excuse. She had been too certain of her own skill and had paid the price for her conceit. The cards had all fallen to Sir Reginald. She could not bear to think of telling Penelope that she had lost her precious brooch, nor could she think of any way to regain it. And it would only be a matter of time until the whole affair came to the ears of Lord Hartford. How grateful he would be then that she had not accepted his proposal. To have a hardened gamester for a wife, one who thought nothing of losing the family jewels! When finally she went to bed, her sleep was haunted by Penelope's sad eyes and Lord Hartford's accusing ones.

Chapter Nine

Before attending Lady Rothmore's party, Lord Hartford found himself obliged to pay a call to Granville House for a private interview with the dowager. He had received her note late in the afternoon, very soon after his arrival from Hartford Park, and he read it with resignation. Soon after dinner he set out for Grosvenor Square, impeccable in satin knee breeches and silk stockings, his chapeau bras under his arm.

"About time you brought yourself back from the country," his aunt said cordially. "You have been needed here."

"Indeed?" he inquired, lifting an eyebrow.

"You needn't act like such a care-for-nobody, Alistair. This is all your fault. How you could have thought it at all the thing to have that heedless Sally chaperone Evan's widow, I cannot think. You most have known that it would bring us to grief."

"I cannot recall that putting Lady Danby in Sally's charge was at all my idea, Aunt, but I daresay that I am forgetting the rights of it. I rather thought you were the one who arranged the matter."

The dowager ignored his remark with magnificent aplomb. "I cannot walk through this house without tripping over some young jackanapes waiting to see her. There is no peace to be had here at all, what with cards and flowers arriving and people going in and out all of the time. Young Ponsonby and his friends were running tame here, but I put them to the rightabout soon enough."

"I can well imagine that you did," remarked her nephew, looking amused. "If she is doing no worse than young Ponsonby, there is little for you to worry about, Aunt."

"Oh, ain't there?" she replied bitterly. "It isn't only young Ponsonby. There's Sir Nevil Graham and Lord Molton and even an old court card like Lord Bartholomew Flanders."

"Does she encourage them, Aunt?" asked Hartford, frowning as Lady Granville named some of Violet's least respectable admirers, annoyed that her actions had the power to concern him.

"Of course she does. The girl encourages everyone. She told me that she wouldn't want to hurt anyone's feelings, so she goes hither and yon with any of the ramshackle fellows she meets at the ton parties. Says if they were invited to the parties, they must be perfectly respectable. Do you know what they are calling her, Alistair?" she demanded. Not waiting for his response, she added, "The Merry Widow! Now isn't that a pretty thing to hear? Next they'll be saying she's a lightskirt and we will all look no-how for having such a skimble-skamble female in the family!"

Lord Hartford gave his aunt a damping look. "You are probably making a great piece of work about nothing, Aunt Maria. I think it would be wise if you did not refer to Lady Danby as a lightskirt."

"So she has taken you in, too, has she?" asked the dowager. "I can almost see why Evan married her. All he saw was her pretty face, just as you do, Alistair. He couldn't have known what a brass-faced hussy she really is." She looked at Hartford bitterly. "She wears the ring and the brooch quite brazenly, you know, but she never wears the other pieces. I asked her one night why she didn't wear a diamond necklace with the gown she was wearing, and she had the audacity to tell me that she did not possess one."

"Perhaps she does not. Sally does not seem to think she is concealing the whereabouts of the other pieces. It could be that Even did not give the other pieces to her."

"More likely that she sold them off to pay for new fripperies," retorted Lady Granville.

"I was under the impression that Lady Danby's uncle left his family well provided for."

"The sherry merchant?" snorted his aunt. "That's as may be. What happened to the other pieces then, Alistair, the necklace and the eardrops and the bracelet? would you have it that your cousin sold them off?"

"Of course not, Aunt. I know that Evan would never have considered doing such a thing."

"Well, where are they then? Answer me that! They weren't with his things in the Peninsula, for those were all brought home to us by his commander. There is no one to have them but his widow."

Lord Hartford took his leave from Granville House in a most unsettled frame of mind. It was impossible to believe that Lady Danby had done anything with the other pieces, but, on the other hand, where could they be? He frowned as he considered the matter. She was young and often distressingly shallow, but surely such a thing as selling her husband's family heirlooms when there was no real need would be beneath her. She wore the ring and brooch quite openly. He wondered again what Evan had told her about the diamonds, for she seemed to feel that they were hers, despite the rather broad hints dropped by the dowager.

Violet dressed carefully for the party that night, feeling that she was about to face her undoing. She knew her case to be hopeless and her usually animated little face was so drained of color that Summers watched her anxiously, unaccustomed to seeing her mistress so blue-deviled. A gown of coral crepe lent some color to her cheeks and a soupçon of rouge did the rest. Summers dressed her hair carefully and fastened a necklace of coral around her throat. Violet sat quite still at the dressing table, submitting to Summers's ministrations with unusual docility, her gaze idly fixed on the top of the dressing table. Her jewel case lay open, a lovely strand of pearls that had been a gift from her aunt lying on the velvet next to the other charming, but less expensive pieces. Her eyes suddenly brightened and she picked them up and regarded them closely.

Some of the idle chatter that she had heard at Lady Mason's had come back to her with new meaning as she sat staring at her jewels. Lady Shelton, the thin, gray-haired woman who regularly staked her necklace at play, had mentioned one day that her late husband had pawned her other jewelry, having gotten himself deep into Dun territory before his death. Violet congratulated herself upon a stroke of brilliance. She had only to discover the whereabouts of such a shop and she could pawn her necklace until the next time she received her allowance. Satisfied, she relaxed and let Summers complete her toilette.

Young Mr. George Ponsonby, Violet's escort for the party, was struck quite dumb when he saw Lady Danby come lightly down the stairs toward him, her piquant face aglow with pleasure. Violet felt as vibrantly alive as one who has been snatched from the very jaws of death, and she was fully prepared to enjoy her evening hugely. She would transact her business tomorrow, after sending a note round to Sir Reginald. She could scarcely wait to tell Sally of her solution.

To her surprise, Lady Sally appeared as radiant as usual at the party. Violet had expected her friend to look cast down by her predicament, but she had no opportunity to satisfy her curiosity until later in the evening, when Lord Hartford and Ponsonby had removed themselves to procure refreshments for the ladies.

Violet quickly confided her idea, but Sally appeared completely disinterested.

"That should serve your purpose very well, Penelope," she remarked absently, "but there is no need for me to resort to such measures."

"Indeed?" asked Violet in astonishment. "Are you no longer afraid that Captain Andrews will approach your brother?"

"He would not dare to," replied Sally with satisfaction, a complacent smile on her lips. "He has received his money and I have the bracelet back again."

"However did you manage that, Sally?"

Her friend's smile widened. "I threw myself upon Sir Geoffrey's mercy and told him the whole of the story. I knew he would not fail me," she said smugly, certain of her charms.

"Sir Geoffrey lent you the money? Are you not afraid of your brother discovering it? He would be quite as angry about your borrowing the money from Sir Geoffrey as he would be that you had lost it to Captain Andrews."

Lady Sally stared coldly at her friend, her eyes narrowing like a cat's. "Alistair will not discover it. Sir Geoffrey would never betray me and you are the only other person who knows how I recovered it. I hope that I have not misplaced my trust, Penelope."

Violet gasped indignantly. "You cannot think that I would do such an unhandsome thing, Sally."

Lady Sally shrugged. "Then there is no problem. And after you take care of the other matter tomorrow, there will be no point in referring to it again."

It was obvious to Violet that Lady Sally felt no responsibility for Violet's present difficulty. And indeed it is my own fault, she reminded herself sharply. Staking Penny's brooch was wrong, no matter what the reasons for doing so. It was clearly not a matter of consequence to Lady Sally that Violet's unhappy situation had come about because of Lady Sally's own heedlessness. Self-absorbed as she had always been, she cared for no one's well-being but her own.

Lord Hartford had an opportunity that evening to see the extent of Lady Danby's popularity, but he could find no fault in her demeanor and meant to inform his aunt of that at the first opportunity. As he led her out to dance, he found himself thinking that she looked uncommonly well and that London was certainly agreeing with her. Their conversation was desultory, interrupted by the movements of the dance, and each was satisfied to have it so. The gentleman was too aware of his own warmth of feeling, and the lady uncomfortably conscious of her own misdeeds.

"You are looking very well, Lady Danby," he commented, thinking privately that she outshone every beauty in the room.

"And you are being very agreeable, Lord Hartford," she returned gaily, acutely aware of how very disagreeable he would be were he to discover her quandary.

"Is it so unusual for me to be agreeable that you must comment upon it?" he inquired in some dismay. "I must be an ogre indeed."

"Not at all, Lord Hartford. It must be tiresome to feel that you are responsible for someone so lacking in judgment as myself. I am certain that you are quite pleasant with your intimates . . ."

Her comment faded as she moved away from Hartford, and when the dance brought her back to his side, he was nettled to see that she was laughing at some sally of Ashby's.

"It is apparent that you find Lord Ashby agreeable." He was annoyed to hear the acidity in his voice and to see that Lady Danby had noticed it.

"Indeed I do, Lord Hartford. He is all that a gentleman should be."

Grateful that the dance separated them once again, Hartford took himself firmly in hand and, when they were united once more, grimly kept the conversation strictly impersonal. When the dance was over, he guided her back to her place, where a gaggle of her admirers waited. Catching a glimpse of Ashby coming towards them, Hartford bowed stiffly and walked away, annoyed for the first time with his friend. He was uncomfortably aware that what he was feeling was very close to jealousy. She was a danger indeed to his peace of mind and peace of mind he was determined to have.

Early the next morning Violet sent a note to Sir Reginald and waited impatiently for his reply, certain that a trip to a pawnbroker's shop would solve her problem. When one of the maid servants brought her the unwelcome information that Lord Hartford had called and was waiting for her in the Red Saloon, Violet made her way downstairs, searching her mind hurriedly for a clue as to the reason for his visit. She had arrived at no satisfactory answer when she entered the room and he rose to greet her. One glance at his face told her everything: the small white lines about his lips revealed how difficult it was for him to hold back his anger, and his voice was like ice.

"I find that we have some private matters to discuss, madam." He reached into the pocket of his coat and drew out Penelope's brooch, handing it to her silently. "Perhaps you will be good enough to give me your own account of how this brooch left your possession."

In a small voice, scrupulously omitting all reference to Lady Sally, Violet told him that she had found herself short of cash and, believing her luck would turn, had staked the brooch.

"I would not have let Sir Reginald keep it though, for I knew that it was not mine to lose." The words seemed to leap from her of their own accord and his eyebrows drew together ominously.

99

"You know that, do you?" he exclaimed harshly. He ran a hand roughly through his hair. "You can imagine my surprise when I received a note this morning from Sir Reginald Hawke, telling me that if I called at his rooms I would learn something of interest regarding a lady in my family. And not only must I learn that my cousin's widow has lost his brooch while gaming, but that she has lost it in play with a man with a devilishly poor reputation, a man about whom she had already been warned."

He turned on her suddenly. "Did you take Sally with you to that place?" he demanded.

Violet shook her head silently. That at least was true. She did not add that it had been Lady Sally who had taken her there initially.

"Well, I am grateful for that at least. Sally may be a goosecap, but she is not so lost to propriety that she would attend a party at an establishment like Mrs. Mason's with such a loose screw as Sir Reginald Hawke."

Violet burned with the injustice of his remark, but she was determined not to be so low as to betray Lady Sally to her brother. She swallowed with difficulty and steadfastly said nothing.

Her silence seemed to enrage him further. "See to it that you keep that brooch safely in your possession, and I do not expect to hear again of your gambling," he said roughly. She nodded and ventured a frightened glance at him.

He stared at her for a long moment, then said in a low voice, "I must know, Lady Danby. Your note to Sir Reginald arrived before I left him and he showed me its contents. How did you expect to redeem the brooch from him when you say that you have no money?"

Violet's voice was very low indeed when she finally spoke. "I had thought to pawn my necklace," she whispered.

Lord Hartford's face was livid. "I should have known!" he said wrathfully. "Doubtless that explains the absence of the other diamonds! My aunt was more discerning than I!"

At this inauspicious moment, before Violet could ask him what he meant, the door opened and Lord Granville strolled into the room. Stopping short at the sight of two angry faces toward him, he raised his quizzing glass to his eye.

"Ah, Hartford. How are you, dear fellow? I beg your pardon for intruding. I had no idea there was anyone here. Just returned to town, you know."

He turned to Violet doubtfully and bowed. "Your servant, ma'am."

Lord Hartford said stiffly, "You remember Lady Danby, Granville."

Lord Granville smiled. "Indeed I do. Most happy to welcome you to Granville House."

Violet stared at him, relieved that he had not given her away, but puzzled just the same. She extended her hand.

"It was most gracious of you to invite me to London, Lord Granville."

"Not at all. I must apologize for being absent, but I had business at Granville Court. I do hope that you are enjoying your stay."

"Very much, sir."

"Allow me to order some refreshments," said Lord Granville, choosing to overlook their flushed, angry expressions.

"I am afraid that I must be leaving, Granville," said Lord Hartford icily. "Ma'am," he said, bowing slightly to Violet.

Violet accorded him the briefest of nods. "Pray do not order anything on my account," she said to Granville. "I have a slight headache and I believe I shall go to my room and rest."

"Very wise, my dear," said her host. "I shall look forward to talking with you when you are feeling better."

Violet sat in her room, distraught and puzzled. Why had Lord Granville seemed to recognize her when he must know that she was not Lady Danby? And there was the business about the diamonds again. Whatever could they be talking about? She certainly could not ask Lord Hartford and she would not ask Lady Granville. She had brought the subject up once with Lady Dora, who had become distressingly nervous and twittery, and begged her not to refer to it again.

Violet sighed. She had made a terrible muddle of everything. Far from making it a simpler matter for Penelope to meet Evan's family, she had made it virtually impossible. I shall go home before I can do any further damage, she decided. For the first time since her arrival in London, the peace of Stanhope Cottage beckoned to her, a safe haven in an increasingly storm-tossed world.

Chapter Ten

By that afternoon, Violet had decided that she must offer an explanation to Bevil St. Clair for her masquerade. She was grateful for his silence and attributed it to his surprise and the confusion and awkwardness of the situation into which he had innocently walked. Seeking him out soon after her solitary nuncheon, she was relieved to find him alone in the library.

"Pray come in, Lady Danby," he invited her smoothly. "Have a seat here next to the fire. The days are grown very chilly."

She seated herself quietly and waited until he ceased bustling about the room, providing a screen to shield her from a quite imaginary draught and ringing for tea. Finally he seated himself in a wing chair facing her own.

"Now, Lady Danby, how may I be of service to you?"

Violet looked at him squarely. "I believe you must know, Lord Granville, that I am not Lady Danby. I am her sister, Violet Carlton."

"I suspected as much," he admitted. "I knew, of

course, that Hartford was going to Bath to fetch you, or rather your sister, for a visit. When I heard that Lady Danby was quite the rage of the ton, heard, in fact that she was being called the Merry Widow by some of the wits, I was quite sure that you were not the Lady Danby that I had met. As I recall," he said thoughtfully, polishing his quizzing glass absently, "Lady Danby is a very shy young woman . . . and a blond. I knew that the Merry Widow was described as a dashing brunette. Since I knew there was a sister, I suspected, of course."

"And you were quite right," replied Violet frankly. "I am not sure why you did not betray me to Lord Hartford, but I am very grateful that you did not."

He chuckled unexpectedly. "I could see that your interview with him was not the happiest one possible. It would hardly have been chivalrous of me to add to your woes."

"It would have been disastrous," Violet admitted. "Do you intend to tell your family the truth now?"

He looked at her curiously. "Could you explain to me the reason for this switching of identities, Miss Carlton?"

"My sister is, as you observed earlier, painfully shy. She was afraid of coming to London, although she felt that it was the proper thing to do," said Violet mendaciously, sacrificing truth to expediency. "We felt that my coming in her place would be preferable to offending her late husband's family."

Lord Granville looked decidedly amused. "And when your visit is over?" he inquired.

"When my visit is over, I will return to Bath and become Violet Carlton once more. Lady Danby will have paid her respects to her husband's family and there need be no further contact between them and us."

Granville's shoulders shook silently. "I would give a monkey to see their faces if they knew the truth." Seeing Violet's startled expression, he held up his hand. "But they will not learn it from me," he reassured her. "I can see no harm in this charade, providing it draws to a close reasonably soon, and it will provide me with infinite pleasure to see my august relatives bamboozled."

Violet looked surprised and he added equably, "My loving family has not always treated me with the greatest kindness, Lady Danby." The malice in his expression was plain. "It will give me a great pleasure to serve them such a backhanded turn as this."

"I give you my thanks again, Lord Granville," she replied coolly, "and I assure you that I will not impose upon your hospitality much longer." Rising, she extended her hand.

"Nonsense, my dear, you need not run away because of me. I did not mean that you must leave immediately. Complete your visit and allow me the enjoyment of watching. As I said before, as long as the masquerade is brought to an end in a reasonable period of time, there is no harm done."

Violet nodded and uneasily removed herself from the library. It was understandable that he would be bitter if he had indeed received Turkish treatment at the hands of his relatives when he was younger, something that she considered entirely possible, but his obvious desire to see them humbled was disturbing. She wondered uncomfortably if he might not find pleasure in exposing her identity himself to enjoy their discomfiture. For the first time, it also occurred to her that Lord Granville might not be best pleased to discover that Evan St. Clair had had a son and she wondered how she could have been such a ninnyhammer as to believe that she could simply tell the dowager about her grandson and that all would then be well. It would undoubtedly be safest to remove herself from London as soon as it was feasible. If she felt any pangs at the thought of leaving, it was because of the pleasures that she would be abandoning, not at all because of a certain high-handed lord.

She had promised to attend Almack's that evening in the company of The Honorable Mr. George Ponsonby, along with Lady Sally and one of her cicisbeos. If the prospect was somewhat less than appealing, she masked her feelings with a gay smile and slipped into a confection of rose satin and lace and dainty Denmark satin sandals, and her escort thought that he had never seen her in greater good looks.

The Honorable Mr. George Ponsonby was a young man of impeccable lineage and, unlike some younger sons, possessed a handsome fortune of his own. He was a dashing young man, a leader among the idle young sparks that so thickly populated the ton, and by becoming the devoted admirer of the Merry Widow, had given greater consequence to them both, for she had quickly been recognized as a noted beauty and he was one of the prizes of the Marriage Mart. Both of them were lively and quick-witted and delighted in the ridiculous, seldom discussing any matter of consequence. Lovely though she was, he was in no danger of losing his heart to her, but they enjoyed one another's company and he was aware that he frequently provided her a refuge from the persistent attentions of her more ardent admirers. Mr. Ponsonby was quite accustomed to lovely young women casting out lures, and he found it agreeably refreshing and relaxing that Lady Danby did not attempt to do so.

He was quick to note that although she looked charming as they prepared to leave Granville House that night, her spirits were low.

"There is no need to go out tonight if you are not feeling quite the thing, Lady Danby," he said gently.

Touched by his quick understanding, she smiled at him gratefully. "Thank you, Mr. Ponsonby, but perhaps it will help if I occupy my mind with something else for a bit. And besides," she added, "Lady Sally is expecting us."

When they arrived at Almack's, the fashionable assembly rooms in King Street, Violet forced herself to smile and move among her admirers in her usual charming manner. She bowed to that capricious leader of the ton, the Countess Lieven, who graciously acknowledged her. In the distance Violet caught a glimpse of Lord Hartford leading a graceful young woman in a white satin gown onto the dance floor. Lady Sally followed her gaze.

"That is Margaret Palmer dancing with Alistair. She has certainly set her cap for him, and I hope that she will attach him. Perhaps if he had a wife of his own to look after, he would have less time for meddling with others." She squeezed Violet's hand and whispered, "I know that he must have given you a shocking scold. He came to see me this afternoon and told me that he was grateful that I had had the good sense not to attend Mrs. Mason's. I *do* thank you, Penelope, for not betraying me."

Violet remained silent, unwilling to continue a conversation on such an unpleasant subject. It seemed not to have occurred to her volatile friend that she could have defended Violet, but then it would not have occurred to Lady Sally that Violet might value Lord Hartford's good opinion. To her relief, Mr. Ponsonby soon led her onto the dance floor, and she was able to regather her thoughts. If the sight of Lord Hartford bending attentively over his dainty partner was a painful one, she could tell herself that it was because it reminded her of their painful interview that morning.

It seemed to Violet that the evening dragged on forever. She did not lack for partners and George Ponsonby was most attentive, but Lord Hartford kept his distance, approaching them only to greet his sister and nod coolly to Violet and Mr. Ponsonby.

While Mr. Ponsonby had gone to fetch her a glass of lemonade a few minutes later, Lady Sally drew her aside to confide in her. "Penelope, I know how you have been longing to attend Vauxhall Gardens and I have quite determined that we shall make up a party and go tomorrow night."

Violet smiled. "That is very kind of you, Sally, but I believe that it is time that I begin to think of returning to Bath."

Lady Sally looked shocked. "You cannot be thinking of going yet, Penelope. Why, you have scarcely arrived."

In amusement Violet reminded her that she had already been in London for several weeks, but Lady Sally waved that aside. "Nonsense. You must stay longer. At any rate, I want to do something for you since you were kind enough to help me. Or at least you tried to help me," she amended. "So you must come to Vauxhall Gardens tomorrow night."

Violet was touched by her friend's effort to be thoughtful. It was unlike Lady Sally to pay much heed to the wishes of others, but it was true that she had mentioned her desire to go to Vauxhall Gardens while in London. She admitted to Sally that it would be very enjoyable.

"Famous!" exclaimed her friend. "Who should I invite as your escort? George Ponsonby?"

Violet nodded. If he were to attend her, that would insure her pleasure in the evening. Lady Sally nodded speculatively. "You and he have become wondrous great, have you not? Oh, I am not prying!" she exclaimed, seeing Violet's eye kindle. "George Ponsonby it shall be then."

The gentleman in question arrived at that point with the lemonade and declared himself more than willing to attend a party at the Pleasure Gardens the next evening. Shortly afterwards, declaring that Lady Danby was worn to a thread, he bore her safely away.

The next day Violet found it difficult to give her thoughts to the evening's expedition, for she found her mind dwelling upon the problems that beset her. The references of both Lord Hartford and the dowager to diamonds, both those she had borrowed from Penelope as well as certain other pieces of which she knew nothing, continued to trouble her, and she decided that she must look into the matter. Careful consideration led her to the conclusion that she could speak most easily to Lord Granville, who already knew the truth of her identity. Accordingly, she sought him out after breakfast and requested a private interview with him in the library. If Lord Granville was startled by the intensity of her tone, he concealed it admirably and led her to his private retreat.

"I fear that I must trespass upon your good nature once again," she began nervously, uncertain of how to begin.

"Nonsense, Lady Danby. I can see that you are troubled, my dear. Pray be seated and tell me how I may serve you."

"Thank you," she replied gratefully, sinking into a chair. "I scarcely know how to begin though," Violet added hesitantly.

"Just pop right out with it," Lord Granville encouraged her. "No need to stand on ceremony."

She drew a deep breath and plunged in. "Very well, sir. Lady Granville and Lord Hartford have both referred to some diamond jewelry that they apparently think I — or rather my sister — possess."

There was a brief silence while they regarded one another intently. "When Evan married Penelope, he presented her with the diamond ring that I wear and the butterfly brooch." She blushed hotly, remembering her interview with Lord Hartford.

"Do you mean to say that's all he gave her?" asked Lord Granville abruptly.

"Yes, of course. What else was there and why do they seem to think Penelope might know of it?"

"There were also a diamond necklace and bracelet and a pair of eardrops — the St. Clair diamonds, they call them. They all disappeared the night young Evan quarreled with his parents over his coming marriage and left Granville Court. They hadn't been seen since then until you arrived here. Except," he amended, "when I called on Lady Danby after the news of Evan's death reached me. She was wearing the brooch and the ring then, and I supposed the other pieces were tucked away somewhere."

He stared at Violet, his eyes shining intently. "Are you certain Evan didn't give the lot to her?"

"Of course I am," said Violet hotly. "Penelope knows nothing about them. He told her that you had been kind enough to ride after him when he left his home that night, and that you had given him the ring and the brooch. He said that you told him his mother had sent them to him secretly."

Lord Granville gave a sudden mirthless crack of laughter. "No such thing! What, the dowager send her precious jewels to the nobody Evan was marrying? I'd like to see it!"

Violet colored again. "I would like to remind you, Lord Granville," she said stiffly, "that you are talking about my sister."

"Beg pardon, my dear. No harm meant. But you must see that ain't likely behavior for Lady Granville."

She nodded slowly, a worried frown creasing her forehead. "I do indeed. You did not tell him that his mother sent them then?"

Lord Granville shook his head emphatically. "Didn't know a thing about them until later, my dear. I went chasing after him to try to convince him to return home, but he would have none of it, so I told him to let me know if ever I could serve him. Then we shook hands and he was gone."

"Then how did he come to have the ring and the brooch?" Violet asked slowly.

The earl looked very uncomfortable. "Well, the plain truth of the matter, my dear, is that the rest of the family believes that he took all of those jewels and presented them to his wife. They would have been his eventually, you know," he added hurriedly, seeing her shocked expression, "when he became the Earl of Granville, and he knew that his mother kept them in a secret drawer in her dressing table. She didn't wear them often, so it would have been several weeks, or even months, before she missed them. I should imagine he just nipped them out and took them along with him."

"And Lord Hartford and Lady Granville believe that Penelope has all of these pieces?"

He nodded. "Can't blame them, you know. What else were they to think?"

"But what could have happened to the other three pieces?"

"He might have sold them," he answered promptly. "My uncle cut Evan off and he could have needed the ready. I offered a roll of soft that night, but he would not take it. Said he had enough."

"Surely he could not have done such a thing, Lord Granville—taking his family jewelry and then selling it, lying to Penelope about his mother sending the ring and the brooch. This would kill my sister if she but knew!"

"Don't tell her," replied Granville helpfully. "No need to."

"No indeed," replied Violet with determination. Penelope would certainly not hear of this from her. She paused—but could Evan have been so very different from what Penelope had believed? The Evan that her

112

sister spoke of would have been incapable of such a dishonorable action. She shook her head slowly. And now his abominable relatives thought that Penelope had all of those family jewels, was keeping them for herself. Her mouth and chin assumed a stubborn set that Mrs. Crawford and Penelope would have recognized immediately and she promised herself that she would unravel this matter.

Lord Granville, less familiar with her, was relieved when she arose and he ushered her from the room with every attention.

"You just put it out of your mind, Lady Danby. Nothing for you to do. That's the ticket! You just smile and enjoy your time here without worrying your head over diamonds."

Unfortunately, Violet could think of little else. Even the greatly anticipated visit to Vauxhall fell sadly flat as she pondered her problem. Lady Sally had arranged a delightful supper in a private booth and George Ponsonby was a most agreeable escort, but Violet could not enter into the fun with the proper spirit.

She was also mildly disturbed by the party itself, having expected a larger group. There were only the four of them, Lady Sally having chosen Sir Geoffrey Hayes as her cicisbeo. Watching her friend flirt outrageously, Violet wondered idly what Lord Hartford would do if he knew about it. At least they were masked, she thought gratefully, as Sir Geoffrey and Lady Sally disappeared down a dark path into the gardens. She and George Ponsonby listened to a portion of the concert, which was devoted to the works of Handel, and then drifted down some of the better-lighted walkways, waiting for the fireworks that would end the festivities.

The ride home was a merry one, at least for Lady Sally and Sir Geoffrey, who appeared to have enjoyed themselves tremendously, but Violet remained absorbed in her own problems, rousing herself only when they reached Granville House. She thanked Sally for the evening and bade good night to Sir Geoffrey before Mr. Ponsonby escorted her to the door.

Chapter Eleven

Among her callers the next morning, Violet was amazed, and not at all pleased, to find Sir Reginald Hawke. His arrival caused a pleasant flurry among the ladies present, Mrs. Cecil Morvel and her two daughters, Rosamund and Celia, for Sir Reginald was quite dashing and had a rakish reputation. The three ladies regarded Lady Danby with somewhat speculative glances. The reason for their morning call was curiosity rather than friendship. Mrs. Morvel was eager to know more about Lady Danby's tragically brief marriage and her daughters were equally eager to study her manner of dress and conversation in the futile hope that they could emulate her success.

Violet had managed to deflect the mother's probing questions, having become quite accustomed to the outrageous curiosity of the ton with regard to its more colorful members. Her surprise at Sir Reginald's entry was evident, and the ladies were hopeful of outstaying him and learning the reason for his call. They were destined to disappointment, however, for his conversation was that of any fashionable gentleman, talk of parties and common acquaintances and such of the latest *on-dits* as were suitable for the ears of young ladies. Propriety strictly dictated the acceptable length of a morning call and the ladies were forced to leave first, abandoning the field to Sir Reginald. Violet had not a doubt that the news of his presence at Granville House would be shared with everyone present at their next destination.

"I am certain that my presence here must surprise you, Lady Danby," said Sir Reginald smoothly as the door closed behind the Morvels.

"I am surprised, and not at all gratified," replied Violet icily. "Your behavior has scarcely been that of a gentleman and I am amazed that you would have the effrontery to address me."

His brief nod acknowledged the justice of her words, but then he smiled ingratiatingly. "Perhaps I can do something to redeem myself in your eyes, Lady Danby."

"I cannot think of any way that you could possibly do so," she answered stiffly, hoping the interview would soon come to an end and unwillingly imagining Lord Hartford's wrath when it came to his ears that she had received Sir Reginald privately.

"Perhaps I can tell you something about your brooch that you did not know."

Thinking of the St. Clair diamonds, she was immediately attentive as well as wary.

"What could you possibly know of jewelry, Sir Reginald?"

"Were you aware, Lady Danby, that your brooch is paste?"

One glance at her startled expression was sufficient

answer. "I thought not," he smiled. "I scarcely thought you would stake it knowing that it was not the real article."

"But it must be real," she said blankly. "The brooch belonged to Evan." Involuntarily she glanced down at the diamond ring she wore.

He followed her glance and said, "Quite so. I should imagine that it is paste also."

"But how could that be? These are Evan's jewels," she repeated.

"Strictly speaking, I would say that they belonged to Evan's father and now belong to Bevil St. Clair," he replied drily.

Her mind whirled. "But Evan gave them to . . . to me."

"From what I know of the business, they were not his to give," said Sir Reginald again. "Of course, there was no way for you to know that . . . unless he told you."

"Of course he did not!" she retorted angrily, flushing at the slur he unwittingly cast upon her sister.

"My apologies, Lady Danby. Of course he did not. One can only wonder why he not only gave you diamonds that were not his to give, but also why he gave you paste rather than the real jewels."

"I cannot imagine why he would do such a thing," said Violet slowly. Then, beginning to regain her composure, she added frostily, "Nor can I imagine why it would be any of your concern, Sir Reginald."

"You forget, madam, that I had a very near interest in the matter when you chose to stake the brooch at Mrs. Mason's. I accepted it under the impression that it was worth a goodly amount, which it certainly is not."

Violet flushed. "But I did think it was, Sir Reginald. There was no deception intended."

He inclined his head graciously. "You and I know that, Lady Danby. Not everyone else is so informed. Your late husband's cousin, for instance. I do not believe that Lord Hartford realized that he was redeeming a paste brooch rather than a diamond one."

Sir Reginald regarded his nails thoughtfully. "It occurs to me, dear lady, that he might not be best pleased if he did know it. He might not understand how it came to be substituted."

"How should he understand it?" asked Violet angrily. "I have no idea how it was substituted myself."

"You and I know that, Lady Danby," he replied pointedly.

Violet flushed again. "Do I understand you to infer, Sir Reginald, that my relatives might believe that I had made the substitution myself?"

He made a slight disclaiming gesture. "It merely appeared to me during my interview with Lord Hartford that your relations with him were, shall we say, a trifle strained."

"That does not mean that he would believe that I would do such a dishonorable thing!"

He smiled at her. "It did not seem to me that he considered gambling away your husband's jewels honorable either, so he might not find it such an impossible thing to believe."

Violet subsided into a fuming silence for a moment. He was all too accurate, of course. Her moment of madness at Mrs. Mason's had sadly reduced what credibility she had had with Lord Hartford. He undoubtedly regarded her capable of any folly.

Her eyes narrowed suddenly as a new thought struck her. "How do I know that you did not make the substitution while it was in your possession?"

He shrugged in a maddeningly unconcerned manner. "You do not, of course, although I assure that I did no such thing."

"But you cannot prove that you did not!" said Violet triumphantly.

"Nor can you, Lady Danby." He looked at her thoughtfully. "May I ask to whom you would report your suspicions of me?"

Violet seethed silently. There was, of course, no one that she could tell. Evan's family would scarcely be pleased to know that the brooch and possibly the ring were paste rather than real, and they certainly did not have such faith in Violet that they would believe that she had had nothing to do with it. Lord Hartford, who set the tone for the others, would find it all too easy to believe. And if Sir Reginald had indeed made the switch, whose fault was it that he had had the brooch in the first place? She was neatly trapped.

"I don't understand, Sir Reginald. I see that this would make an interesting piece of gossip, but what other good would this knowledge do you?"

He smiled at her unpleasantly. "I was waiting for you to ask, Lady Danby. I would not, of course, wish to cause a lady any unnecessary discomfort. You may be certain that I will mention this to no one, provided . . ."

"Provided what?" broke in Violet when he paused too long.

"Provided that you occasionally give me the plea-

119

sure of your company, Lady Danby."

She stared at him in disbelief. "Whatever for?" she asked. "You cannot pretend that you have a *tendre* for me."

"You wrong me, Lady Danby," he protested. "I find you most attractive. If you would but do me the occasional honor of spending an evening with me, I feel that we may put this unpleasant business out of our minds."

"I don't understand at all, and I cannot pretend to like it," she replied frankly, "but I cannot see that I have any choice."

He bowed gracefully to her. "As you say, Lady Danby, there is little choice. Let us hope that you will feel more kindly toward me after spending some time in my company." And he quietly started toward the door, pausing just before he opened it.

"Shall we say au revoir until this evening?" he inquired. "I had thought that after dinner you might like to look in on a small party at Mrs. Mason's."

Violet opened her mouth to make an angry denial, but his quizzically upraised eyebrow reminded her of her situation. She swallowed and said in a small voice, "Very well, Sir Reginald."

He smiled approvingly and departed, leaving Violet caught between anger at his impudence and mounting fear over her predicament. Why would a man like Sir Reginald want her company? She knew that she was correct in believing that his heart was not engaged. Why this interest in the diamonds? Could he believe, like the others, that Lady Danby had all of the St. Clair diamonds?

Most earnestly she wished that there were someone

120

in London to whom she could turn for help. Lady Dora had shown her the greatest kindness, but she could not for a moment imagine sharing this problem with her. She paused. Perhaps Lord Granville. He had been most obliging and had kept her secret. Violet smiled in sudden relief. She would most certainly consult him at the first possible moment.

To her dismay, however, she found that Lord Granville had gone out and was not expected in until very late that evening. She would have no choice but to go with Sir Reginald tonight. Briefly she toyed with the idea of pleading illness, but she had no confidence in his ability to command his temper. He might very well seek Lord Hartford out immediately and share this latest unpalatable information with him.

Even though she dressed carefully in a most becoming dress of black crepe over a black sarsnet slip, Violet's spirits remained depressed. It was all very well for Summers to sniff smugly that her gown would set the fashion and that there would be a flurry of calls to Madame Celeste after the ladies of the ton saw Lady Danby in her newest creation. Violet could take no comfort from such fripperies tonight. She listened absently as Summers pointed out the finer points of her dress: the rouleau of crepe intermixed with jet beads that trimmed the low, square neckline; the new elegant half sleeves that began low on her white shoulders; the scalloped hem ornamented with narrow black fancy trimming and an embroidery of crepe roses. Languidly she watched as the abigail fastened in place her headdress, an elegant jet rose and an aigrette, from which a long black veil floated behind her. Her necklace and earrings were of jet and her chamois leather gloves and shoes were also black.

I both look and feel quite like a widow now, she thought miserably. And not at all a merry one. She drifted quietly down the stairs to pay her respects to the dowager and Lady Dora before going out, acutely aware that they would scarcely approve of a man like Sir Reginald Hawke as her escort.

"Why, how very lovely you look, Penelope," twittered Lady Dora as she entered the drawing room.

"Almost like a widow!" exclaimed the dowager, snorting at her own pleasantry. "Pity you don't act more like one!"

Lady Dora frowned at her sister and addressed herself to Violet. "Are you expecting George Ponsonby, Penelope? Such a very nice young man. I was so fond of his dear mother."

Violet shifted uncomfortably, thinking of the note she had sent to George. She had pleaded an indisposition to avoid attending the theatre with him.

"No, Lady Dora. I am expecting Sir Reginald Hawke."

Lady Dora's eyes widened and she glanced apprehensively at her sister, who was swelling visibly.

"I might have known that a gentleman like Ponsonby would not do for you. Sir Reginald Hawke! How gratifying to know that my son's widow will be spending the evening with a rake-shame like that! May I ask where you will be going?"

"I believe that we will be attending a party at the home of one of Sir Reginald's friends," replied Violet in a low voice.

"Friends!" the dowager sniffed derisively. "Any friends that he has will be of the same cut, so you'll no doubt be spending the evening in charming company. If you didn't have more hair than wit, you'd avoid hedge-birds like Reginald Hawke."

Violet could think of nothing to say, so she preserved a discreet silence, allowing Lady Granville's wrath to run its course. She noticed that not even Lady Dora could think of a kindly remark to make about Sir Reginald. When the dowager paused to draw a breath, Violet said hurriedly, "I believe I forgot something in my room. If you will excuse me, I will bid you both good-night now."

She encountered Ruffing in the hall and asked him to show Sir Reginald to the morning room when he arrived. At least she would not have to encounter Lady Granville's acid tongue again this evening, although she would doubtless be subjected to it tomorrow morning.

Sir Reginald was as polished and urbane as ever and Violet reflected that, if one knew nothing of him, he would appear to be as charming an escort as a woman could desire. She discovered that Mrs. Mason's evening parties catered to a different clientele; there were more gentlemen than ladies present and the play was deeper. Sir Reginald introduced her to a number of his friends, procured for her a glass of champagne and a small gilt chair upholstered in straw-colored satin, seated himself at a nearby table, and quickly became absorbed in play.

Violet drew her chair into the shadow of a potted palm and tried to conceal herself as much as possible. She had noted the raised eyebrows as one or two of the gentlemen had recognized her. Very few of the people present were known to her and the ones that were belonged to a very fast set. It was certainly no place for a lady who wished to maintain her reputation. As she listened to the snatches of conversation that floated by her, she realized with horror that upstairs the gentlemen were playing at the E.O. tables and that Mrs. Mason's home was actually a very plush gaming hell. Small wonder that Lord Hartford had been so angry that she had attended such a place.

The evening seemed to last forever. Violet picked at the cold salmon that Mrs. Mason brought to her and drank another glass of champagne. Occasionally she found herself the target of unwanted attentions from unknown gentlemen and burned with embarrassment. Sir Reginald seemed to have forgotten her presence and she wondered miserably how long she would have to remain. At least being ignored was better than his embarrassing attentiveness when they first met, she reflected wryly.

"Lady Danby!"

Violet jumped and glanced up fearfully. She had hoped to see no one that she knew well, but Lord Ashby quietly drew up a chair at her side.

"Lady Danby, don't wish to interfere. None of my business, of course. Just a word though. Not the thing for you to be here."

"I know, Lord Ashby." Her eyes suddenly filled and threatened to overflow. "I did not realize that Mrs. Mason ran a gaming house, or I never would have agreed to come here. I thought she just had parties."

Ashby nodded. "Didn't think you knew. Not the thing at all for a lady." He paused a moment, thinking. "Alistair wouldn't like it at all. Well, dash it, I don't like it above half myself. Why are you sitting here alone?"

Violet nodded toward Sir Reginald, who was deeply absorbed in his game and had not noticed Ashby's arrival. "I came with Sir Reginald, but he has become quite caught up in his playing."

Ashby's slightly protuberant blue eyes almost started from their sockets. "Sir Reginald Hawke?" He shook his head. "Told Alistair he had best keep an eye on you. Not up to snuff at all. No wish to offend, Lady Danby," he added hurriedly, "not the least."

Tears ran down Violet's cheeks. "I am not offended, Lord Ashby. How could I be when what you say is so obviously true? If I had known what o'clock it is, I never would have found myself in this dreadful mess."

Lord Ashby watched her with a worried eye. "Now, now, no need to turn into a watering-pot. We'll fix it up all right and tight."

"How? What can you do to help me, Lord Ashby?"

"Take you home, Lady Danby," he answered simply. "Take you back to Granville House."

"But what of Sir Reginald?" she exclaimed, "Won't he object?"

"If he even notices, which is more than I bargain for, I should like to see him object," he replied pugnaciously. "Ought to have his cork drawn for bringing a young female to such a place as this."

Lord Ashby was as good as his word. He bundled Violet hastily down the front stairs and into his waiting carriage.

"I cannot thank you enough, Lord Ashby," she said gratefully as she sank back against the seat.

"Glad to be of service. No need to mention this to anyone, you know." He looked at her worriedly. "Not the thing, you know, Lady Danby," he repeated.

"You need not worry. I will not go back to Mrs. Mason's, nor do I wish for Sir Reginald's company." She was careful in her choice of words, fearing that she might indeed have to go out with Sir Reginald again, but she could hardly explain that to Lord Ashby.

He heaved a sigh of relief. "That's all right, then. Plenty of other things to do," he said encouragingly. "Go out with that Ponsonby or one of the other beaux that follow you about like puppies."

They drew up in front of Granville House and she laughed as she gave him her hand. "I do thank you most sincerely, Lord Ashby. Your behavior was very gallant."

He drew back, visibly embarrassed. "Nonsense. Glad to be of service."

Violet breathed more easily when she was back in the safety of her own room. Grateful as she had been to escape from Mrs. Mason's, she knew that she could expect an ugly confrontation with Sir Reginald tomorrow. He would scarcely be pleased that she had left with Ashby, although she had certainly served no purpose sitting alone as she had throughout the evening. Again she wondered why he had insisted upon her presence.

Chapter Twelve

The answer to Violet's question was not long in coming. Scarcely had she risen from the breakfast table when Ruffing announced in funereal tones that Sir Reginald Hawke desired to speak to Lady Danby privately. Violet spoke hastily, forestalling the dowager.

"Show him into the morning room, Ruffing. I shall join him right away." With little more than a glance for her two startled aunts, Violet hurried from the room.

"A private meeting, indeed!" exclaimed the dowager angrily. "Such impudence! Under my very roof!"

"I am sure that there is nothing wrong," said Lady Dora pacifically, although she looked worried. "Not as discreet as one might like, of course, but I cannot believe that Violet would be involved in anything clandestine. Her nature is too open."

Her sister snorted. "I have no patience with your soft-heartedness, Dora. You would shed tears over the devil because he can't get into heaven. It is bad enough that she sees that man at all, but she shan't be permitted to see him under my roof!"

She drew herself erect and, cane in hand, sailed toward the morning room. "I shall soon put a stop to this pretty business!" she announced to Dora.

As Violet had feared, she found Sir Reginald in a black humor.

"I understand that Ashby escorted you home last night," he said briefly, dispensing with the formality of a greeting.

"That is correct."

"Is it not your custom to allow the gentleman who takes you out also to see you home? Or is that not the custom in the country?" he sneered.

"Had my escort last night been a gentleman, there would have been no need for Lord Ashby to see me home as he very kindly did. You, I noted, were otherwise occupied," she replied coolly.

"Of course I was occupied. That is why I attended. I told you that we were to have a business arrangement. You cannot expect to have all of the social graces observed in such a situation."

"I am a lady and I expect to be treated as such," she snapped. "As for our 'business arrangement,' as you call it, I can see no point to it at all. I simply sat like a stone for the entire evening. What possible purpose could that serve?"

"You were seen, my dear, as I intended that you should be," he replied.

She looked at him blankly. "And of what use is that?"

He smiled, and she found his smile singularly frightening. "You are too modest, Lady Danby. Where the Merry Widow goes, her train of admirers is sure to follow. After you have spent two or three evenings at Mrs.

Mason's establishment, the word will be out, and there will be a group of young fledglings ready for plucking within our grasp."

She gasped as his meaning became clear to her. "Do you mean to say that you would use me to draw young men like George Ponsonby there and you would lure them into playing and losing their money?"

He smiled again. "It is always possible that they might win. Very unlikely, I admit, but possible. You must realize, though, that I am greatly in need of money at the moment, so I do not believe I could allow them to do so."

"But that is despicable! How can you believe that I would be party to such an infamous scheme?"

"You have no choice, Lady Danby. If you recall, you are most unwilling to have your late husband's family know that the St. Clair diamonds have magically been turned to paste."

Violet had no chance to respond, for at this moment the door of the morning room opened and Lady Granville entered unannounced.

"Lady Granville, I would like to present Sir Reginald Hawke," said Violet stiffly.

The dowager waved her hand disparagingly. "I know who he is, girl, I knew his father, too, and if what I hear of this one is true, there is not a pennysworth to choose between them."

"You do me honor, ma'am," said Sir Reginald. "I am held to be very like my father, I believe."

"Shouldn't brag about it, if I was you," snapped the dowager. "Not to wrap it up in clean linen, he was a loose screw if ever there was one."

Sir Reginald's face darkened ominously, but she

gave him no time to reply. Jabbing in his direction with her cane, she demanded, "What I want to know is what is your business with my son's widow?"

"That is, I fear, a private matter, Lady Granville," he replied smoothly, although his expression was still threatening.

"Nonsense! I will have the truth!" She turned to Violet. "You tell me then. Why is this man here?"

"He came to apologize, Lady Granville. We had a slight misunderstanding last night."

"Came to apologize, did he?" she asked, looking at Violet sharply. "I didn't cut my eye teeth yesterday, so don't be thinking it! I know there's something havey-cavey going on and I want it stopped." She thumped her cane on the floor for emphasis. "Lady Danby, I do not want you seeing this . . . gentleman. Do I make myself clear?"

Violet nodded, her eyes downcast. Satisfied, she turned to Sir Reginald. "Ruffing will show you out, Sir Reginald."

He bowed to Lady Granville and said in a voice thickened by emotion, "I can only trust that I will be able to gaze upon Lady Danby from afar—"

"Stuff!" said the dowager briefly and opened the door to the morning room in a pointed gesture. Violet heard him walk out and did not dare to lift her eyes to encounter his gaze.

When Violet heard the door close, she looked up to find herself alone in the room. Limp with emotion, she collapsed into the nearest chair. She knew, of course, that the aunts disliked the idea of her seeing Sir Reginald, but she had been completely unprepared for such a scene as the one that she had just witnessed.

130

What could he have done to earn such a set-down from Lady Granville? And what must she think of her daughter-in-law? Violet closed her eyes. It seemed as though everything that she did led her more deeply into trouble. Never would she be able to explain it to Penelope.

However could she tell Penelope that her precious diamonds were paste and that Evan must have been responsible for the substitution, as well as the loss of the other pieces of the set? Her sister would never accept such an accusation against her dead husband. She knew very well that Penelope had considered him the essence of all that was honorable and would be outraged by even a suggestion of wrongdoing. Violet considered the matter carefully. Could he have hidden the diamonds for some reason? He and Penelope had spent a week at Stanhope Cottage after their marriage, but Violet could think of no hiding places there that would have remained secure for three years. Aunt Serena was too meticulous a housekeeper to allow small cubbyholes to remain uncleaned for more than a matter of weeks. And, if he had hidden something, why had he not told Penelope? Violet shook her head. Nothing made any sense.

Finally she stood up resolutely. She would talk to Lord Granville. Perhaps he could help her with part of her dilemma at least.

She once more found him cozily ensconced in his library and he looked up from his book with a welcoming smile, which changed to a look of concern when he saw her expression.

"Come in and sit down, cousin," he said, rising from his chair to pull one closer to the fire for her. "Let me

131

ring for some tea."

Violet made no move to stop him. A cup of tea would be more than welcome. Perhaps it would help to calm her nerves.

"It is plain that you are upset. How may I help you?"

She smiled up at him, grateful for his calm good sense. "It is quite a muddle, I'm afraid," she answered. "I have found myself in a most unpleasant position."

She stopped, hating to expose her own folly, but he looked at her encouragingly and she continued.

"The worst part of it is that I brought it all upon myself." Quickly she explained her trips to Mrs. Mason's, again omitting all reference to Lady Sally, and told him of the fateful afternoon when she had staked the brooch and lost it to Sir Reginald.

"To Sir Reginald Hawke?" he interrupted incredulously.

Violet nodded, her cheeks crimson. "And before I could reclaim it, he revealed it to Lord Hartford."

"And then you were in the basket," remarked her enthralled audience.

"I certainly was, to say the least. Lord Hartford was displeased."

"I can well imagine that displeased was a very mild term for his condition," chuckled Lord Granville.

Violet bit her lip, wishing that he were not enjoying the tale of woe quite so obviously.

"But that was not the worst of it," she continued resolutely.

"You don't mean there's more!" he exclaimed.

"Sir Reginald came to call on me the very next morning and told me that the brooch was paste, not real stones."

Lord Granville sat up very straight at this. "Paste? The butterfly brooch?"

Violet nodded miserably. "I told him that I knew nothing of it, but he pointed out that no one would be likely to believe me and that if he were to tell Lord Hartford and Lady Granville, they would very likely believe that I made the substitution for my own benefit. But neither I nor Penelope would do such a thing, Lord Granville. I thought that perhaps since you had been so kind, you might believe me."

He nodded almost absently. "Yes, I do believe you, my dear. But how very extraordinary! And what did Sir Reginald want of you in return for his silence?" he asked, his voice sharpening.

"I am mortified to have to tell anyone what he wanted," she replied, her eyes lowered. "He said that since I have been fortunate enough to attract some young admirers, he wanted me to come with him to Mrs. Mason's so that they would come, too."

"And he would take them very neatly," finished Lord Granville grimly. "Yes, that sounds quite like Sir Reginald."

"I had to go with him last night. You were not here so that I could talk to you first. It was a most miserable evening and when Lord Ashby offered to bring me home, I allowed him to do so. Sir Reginald was furious and when he called this morning, there was a most lowering scene between him and Lady Granville. She ordered him out of the house and told him that he was not to see me again."

"No, did she really? How famous! I wish that I could have seen his face!"

"He was furious and I was ready to sink for shame.

But the curious thing about it, Lord Granville, is that she did not even know of last night when she was so angry." She paused hesitantly. "It was as though she were angry with him for some other reason."

"She certainly had another reason," replied Lord Granville drily. "It is not well known, but shortly before the late Lord Danby met your sister, he became embroiled with Sir Reginald and his little group. I know that he lost at least ten thousand pounds to Sir Reginald, probably because Sir Reginald fuzzed the cards, and there is no telling what else he might have lost of which I did not hear. His father hushed up the whole affair pretty thoroughly. That is when Evan was exiled to the country for a repairing lease and met your sister. Out of the frying pan into the fire, as they say," he added, grinning.

Violet chose to overlook his reference to Evan's marriage and remained absorbed in thought for a moment. That was how she had lost the brooch then — not in fair play, but because Sir Reginald was a cheat.

"Have you any suggestion as to what I should do, Lord Granville?" she asked slowly. "It seems to me from what you have said that it is possible that Evan might have sought Sir Reginald out after taking the jewels and tried to redeem his losses."

There was a silence while each of them considered the matter and then she asked hesitantly, "Could it be that he might have taken the diamonds earlier and substituted paste replicas for the real ones to fund his gaming? I should hate to think that of him, but young men are sometimes wild, I know, and he was very young."

Bevil nodded slowly. "He was indeed. There could

be a great deal of truth in what you say although I had never considered the possibility before."

"But how distressing for my sister if she were to know of it! Such a lowering reflection to think that he might have done such a thing. Lady Granville would never believe it of her son, I am sure, and would still believe that Penelope was responsible for both the missing jewels and the paste substitution. There is no proof!"

"I am afraid not, my dear," said Lord Granville regretfully. "The only way to prove it would be to regain the original jewels."

Violet's eyes suddenly brightened. "Of course! That is the answer! We must recover the jewels!"

"I beg your pardon?" said Lord Granville, startled by her outburst.

"From what you have told me, it seems quite possible that Sir Reginald might have won the diamonds from Evan. Would he be likely to sell them?"

"Hardly," remarked Bevil. "They would be recognized if he were to try to do so, and even though he may have won them at play, there would be a most unpleasant scene. Of course," he added thoughtfully, "he may have removed some of the stones from their settings, but they are worth a great deal more as they are. I expect he would have to leave the country to sell them, and to my knowledge he has not done so."

"Then we might be able to regain them."

"How?" he inquired curiously.

"If I were to go with him to Mrs. Mason's again, I might be able to get him to play at piquet with me again. I shall supply my own cards this time," she added. "I believe that I would be quite good enough to defeat him if he is not allowed to cheat."

"You would be?" he asked in surprise. "You are a constant source of amazement, Lady Danby. May I ask how you would get him to wager the jewels?"

"By winning," she replied simply. "He told me this morning that he is at Point Non Plus. He will play with me because I will tell him that my aunt, who is a very wealthy woman, has sent me a great deal of money as a gift. He will not be able to resist so easy a mark, and if I can secure just one of the other pieces, I shall have evidence that we are right."

"And has your aunt sent you money?" he asked curiously.

"No," she replied frankly. "I was hoping, Lord Granville, that you might let me borrow it from you."

He burst into laughter. "How could I refuse? It is quite irresistible! Although, to be quite honest with you, I have little enough ready cash until the solicitors have settled the estate. Tell me, though, aside from supplying your own playing cards, how will you keep him from cheating?"

"I shall take a watchdog," Violet answered briskly, quickly laying her plans. "I shall take someone in whom I can trust and have him stand close beside Sir Reginald so that he will not dare to cheat."

"And have you chosen your watchdog?"

"I have. I shall ask Lord Ashby to come with me. He is quite familiar with gaming and no mean player himself, I know that I can trust him."

"But will he agree to do it?"

"He will not wish to, but he is too much the gentleman to refuse me."

"Lady Danby, I salute you," he said sincerely. "I do

indeed believe that you may bring Sir Reginald neatly to account. I am grateful that I am not in his place."

Violet smiled, feeling like herself again for the first time in weeks.

Chapter Thirteen

Violet might have felt that her day had held quite enough excitement already, but she soon discovered that there was much more to come. She retired to her room to formulate her strategy for entrapping Sir Reginald, and had scarcely settled herself in an easy chair to think when Lady Dora tapped softly at the door.

"Excuse me, Penelope dear, but I felt that I must come and talk to you privately for a moment." After patting Violet on the shoulder, she seated herself daintily on the edge of the chair of the dressing table.

"I know that you have had an amazingly unpleasant morning, and I came to tell you how very sorry I am."

"Thank you, Lady Dora," said Violet warmly, "but it had nothing to do with you. There's no need for you to apologize."

"Well, I feel that I must explain a little about Maria." She looked at Violet closely. "I'm afraid that we should have mentioned the matter sooner, but I had no idea that it would possibly come up. About Sir Reginald, I mean."

Violet felt remarkably uncomfortable. She knew

that Lady Dora was referring to the matter with Evan, but she could not tell her that she already knew of the incident, so she was forced to let her proceed.

"Dear Evan was a very high-spirited boy, and sometimes, you know, boys do things very hastily and do not consider the consequences." She paused. "I'm afraid that it was that way with Evan when he became involved with Sir Reginald. He lost a quite large amount of money to Sir Reginald just before he met you, my dear. I do not think that Sir Reginald won fairly. That is rather a harsh thing to say of anyone, but that is his reputation. At any rate, Evan's father was terribly angry and sent Evan away for a while. It was only a few weeks after that when he was so fortunate as to meet you."

She looked at Violet wistfully. "You can see, I think, why Maria was so particularly upset when you chose to go out with Sir Reginald, although I know that she did not handle it well at all."

"Pray don't give it another thought, Lady Dora. I have put it out of my mind."

"Thank you, my dear." She smiled gently. "It is not delicate of me to mention this perhaps, but I cannot help thinking that it might have made a difference if you and Evan had had a child. For your sake certainly, but for Maria's, too. She still feels Evan's loss dreadfully. A child would have given her something to live for. But there, I've said too much," she broke off, seeing Violet's uncomfortable expression. "You must forgive an old lady for running on, my dear."

Violet sat quietly for a few moments after Lady Dora slipped out of the room. She felt that there was a great deal of truth in her observations about Lady

Granville, but how would she feel about having a grandson who came complete with a mother? Violet was not sure that it would work out. And at any rate, she thought, for the moment I am still Lady Danby and I have some problems to unravel.

Just before going down to the dining room for nuncheon, Violet received a note from Lady Sally, announcing that she would not be able to go shopping that afternoon. She was not feeling at all well and planned to stay home and rest in preparation for the Rushmore soirée that evening. Violet heaved a sigh of relief. That would be one less problem to deal with, for she did not have time for Sally that afternoon. She had already sent a note of her own to Lord Ashby, asking him to take her for a drive in the Park that afternoon as she had a private matter to discuss with him. Her message to Sir Reginald had been delivered at the same time, and Violet had offered to play him for her freedom, using the money sent by her aunt as the bait.

The three ladies shared a light repast of cold meats and fruit alone, for Lord Granville had gone out for the afternoon. Violet had dreaded seeing Lady Granville again, but the dowager made no reference to the events of the morning, contenting herself with only an occasional animadversion on the shortcomings of the younger generation. Before Violet could escape again to the safety of her room, however, Ruffing announced that Lord Hartford would like a word with her in the drawing room.

"Alistair?" asked the dowager querulously. "I suppose he came to see me, Ruffing. You may show him in."

"I beg your pardon, Your Ladyship, but Lord Hartford was quite particular in his message. He wishes to speak to Lady Danby."

The dowager fixed her with a baleful eye for a moment and then laughed. "I fancy that you have already heard what he is going to tell you now, Lady Danby. I wish you the pleasure of it."

Violet, who felt that this would be a much more harrowing interview than the one with the dowager and Sir Reginald, was not cheered by her malevolent laughter, and she walked down the hall to the drawing room as though it were Tyburn Road. A single glance at Lord Hartford's face as she closed the door was enough to confirm her worst fears.

"I understand, Lady Danby, that I shall have to thank Lord Ashby for his good offices in removing you from a gaming hell last night." He looked as though he had been carved from ice, and his tone was as cold. Violet felt chilled to the very bone.

"I have already thanked him, Lord Hartford," she replied calmly, clasping her hands tightly together.

"I find it curious, madam, that your escort did not choose to see you home himself."

"My escort was . . . otherwise engaged, Lord Hartford."

His icy composure suddenly dissolved and he turned on her in a black rage.

"How is it, Lady Danby, that you were in the very place I told you to avoid, in company with the man I told you it would be best not to see? Have you so little regard for your reputation that you would throw it away with both hands?"

"Is my reputation quite gone then?" she asked quietly.

Infuriated by her composure, he replied bitterly. "It soon will be, madam, if you persist in this folly. It almost seems to me that you deliberately do the very thing that I recommend you avoid doing."

"I assure you that is not the case, sir, although I must confess I have frequently felt that way when you deliver your ultimatums without a word of explanation. I am not a child, you know."

He stared at her. "What do you mean?"

"You could have told me that it would be best that I not see Sir Reginald Hawke because my . . . husband was involved in an unpleasant incident with him."

"You have heard about that?"

She nodded. "Lady Granville was gracious enough to order him from this house in my presence, although I did not know the true reason for her action until later."

"Perhaps I should have told you, Lady Danby, in which case I must apologize," he said stiffly. "If I have seemed overbearing, I assure you that I had only your own best interests at heart."

Violet had prepared herself for anger and contempt, but she found herself singularly unequipped to deal with kindness. She knew that she could not allow him to talk with her calmly. Far better if he were to stay angry, for what she was about to do would infuriate him far more when he heard of it.

Accordingly, she merely received his apology silently, only inclining her head to show that she had heard him. A lengthy silence ensued until at last Violet was driven to look directly at him. She was dismayed to see that his expression had softened and that he was watching her closely.

"Again, Lady Danby, I must ask your forgiveness. I do forget your youth and inexperience, for you seem to go on so well in the ton. Enough has been made of this matter."

He paused, waiting for her response. Violet bit her lip to keep back the tears. It would have been a great relief to tell him the truth, but she had Penelope and Evan of which to think.

Seeing her distress, Hartford took a step closer and said gently, "Could you not give me the right to look after you, Lady Danby? You said that we would not suit, but I would be willing to try."

Violet turned away from him abruptly so that he would not see the tears spilling down her cheeks. Afraid to trust her voice, she shook her head.

His face darkened as she turned away. "Very well. Forgive me for raising again a subject painful to us both."

Taking a step toward her, he continued, "I would hope that you would avoid both Sir Reginald and Mrs. Mason's establishment for the sake of your own name. You know them both now for what they are."

He stirred uneasily when she remained silent.

"Have you nothing further to say on the matter, Lady Danby?"

She shook her head. "I cannot think what it would be, Lord Hartford."

"You could say that you will have nothing more to do with either Sir Reginald or Mrs. Mason. Can you do so?"

When she maintained her silence, his mouth tightened ominously. "Very well. I quite understand. You do plan to see them and will pay no heed to my coun-

143

sel."

He bowed to her ironically. "It has been my pleasure to speak with you, Lady Danby. Allow me to wish you the good fortune that you will assuredly need since you plan to continue your acquaintance with that pretty pair."

He left the room quickly, closing the door sharply behind him. Violet sank down on the sofa, drained of all emotion. It could not matter what Lord Hartford thought of her. She must keep him at a safe distance while she put her plan into action.

Remembering that she needed to purchase some new piquet packs, she hurriedly changed into a carriage dress and ordered the barouche. As she passed Lady Sally's town house, she saw her walking lightly down the front stairs, her arm linked confidingly with that of her escort, Sir Geoffrey Hayes. So deep in conversation were they that neither one of them took note of Violet passing by. She had no time to think of anyone's problems but her own, but the sight of the couple so obviously oblivious to everyone else troubled her. Sternly she put it from her mind and concentrated on her plan.

While purchasing her cards, a shelf of toys behind the counter caught her eye and she thought guiltily of Penelope and Evan.

"I have a nephew just three years of age," she told the clerk. "What would you suggest as a gift?"

In reply, the clerk took down a brightly colored top and, setting it on the counter, spun it. Delighted by its rainbow blur of brightness, she placed it with her other purchases, adding a book for Penelope and a piquet pack for Mrs. Crawford. She walked swiftly back to the waiting carriage, taking no note of the small, dark man who had been standing next to her at the counter.

Lord Ashby called on her promptly at five o'clock, an apprehensive expression on his usually amiable face. Violet would have found it amusing had she not been so engrossed in explaining her plan, or at least a greatly abridged version of her plan, to him. Her explanation plainly did little to allay his fears.

"My apologies, Lady Danby. Couldn't have heard you just right. Don't suppose that you said you're going back to Ellen Mason's tonight?" He watched her hopefully, waiting for her denial.

When she confirmed his statement, his face fell ludicrously. "Out of the question. Not the place for a lady. Told you so." He looked at her desperately.

"But I told you, Lord Ashby, I must return there. Sir Reginald has something of mine and I mean to reclaim it."

"Tell you what. Tell me what it is and I'll go round and pick it up for you," he said hopefully.

She shook her head. "He won't give it to you nor to me. I shall have to win it back."

Lord Ashby paled visibly. "Win it back?" he asked feebly. "Can't mean to play there, can you?"

"Indeed I shall and, with your help, I will beat him and regain my property."

"My help?" croaked Ashby. "Always glad to be of assistance, Lady Danby, but — "

Violet cut him off ruthlessly. "That is why I turned to you, Lord Ashby," she said appealingly. "I knew that you would not let me go to that place alone."

"Alone? I should say not! Not the place for a young female to go jauntering off to alone. Not the place for a young female at all," he added hastily, seeing too late the trap into which he was falling.

"But I must, Lord Ashby. I have no choice." She paused dramatically. "You would not wish to see me ruined, would you, sir?"

"Ruined? Dash it all, if I take you there, you jolly well will be ruined and so will I if ever Alistair hears about it, and he will."

"Then I fear that I must indeed go alone," Violet said in a sad little voice, looking down at her neatly gloved hands.

"I say, Lady Danby, you can't do that. You can't go alone."

She clasped her hands together joyfully. "I knew that you were too kind to allow me to do so!" she exclaimed. "How shall I ever be able to thank you?"

Lord Ashby's shirt points had wilted visibly by the time he had delivered her safely back to Granville House. Most unwillingly he agreed to call for her at ten o'clock and promised faithfully to keep a wary eye on every move made by Sir Reginald during their game. He drove briskly away, trying not to imagine what scathing things Alistair would have to say to him when next they met.

Chapter Fourteen

When Violet entered Mrs. Mason's that evening with an unhappy Lord Ashby in her wake, Sir Reginald was awaiting her. He looked uneasily at Ashby, but smiled and bowed politely to Violet.

"I am delighted to see you, Lady Danby. If you will come with me, I have taken the liberty of setting our table in an alcove which will be a bit more private."

"How very kind, Sir Reginald," murmured Violet, following him to a small recess screened by potted palms. Lord Ashby walked behind them resolutely.

"I know that you are far fonder of faro than piquet, Ashby," Sir Reginald said easily. "I fear that we will bore you dreadfully, so please feel free to join the others upstairs."

"Not at all, Sir Reginald," he replied politely. "I assure you that I am looking forward to this game with great anticipation."

"In that case," said his host smoothly, "allow me to bring us all a glass of champagne."

Lord Ashby allowed himself the merest wisp of a grin as Sir Reginald walked away to find the champagne. "Dashed unhappy to see me here, ain't he? Looks blue as megrim. May enjoy this more than I thought to." His grin suddenly disappeared as he had another thought. "As long as Alistair don't find out, that is. Might feel obliged to darken my daylights for me."

"There is no reason for him to find out," said Violet comfortingly. "After all, almost no one saw us enter and even if he should find out, I would tell Lord Hartford that I forced you to do this."

"Should have stopped you. Not the place for you at all," he fretted.

"You know that I would have come anyway, Lord Ashby. You were merely playing the part of a gentleman and protecting me."

Fortunately, Sir Reginald made his appearance at that moment and Lord Ashby had no more time to repine, for he was beginning to feel that he had been gulled and would never be able to explain his actions to any reasonable human being. As one of the fashionable leaders of the ton, he quailed to think of the possible consequences of this outrageous breach of etiquette.

"You understand, Sir Reginald, that if I should win our game tonight, you give me your word as a gentleman that I am no longer under any obligation to you," began Violet in a businesslike tone, avoiding Lord Ashby's eye.

Lord Ashby, torn between his horror at hearing Violet announce that she was under an obligation to Sir Reginald and his doubt as to whether or not Sir Reginald was entitled to give his word as a gentleman, stared at Violet with glazed eyes. He had stepped into deep waters indeed!

Sir Reginald nodded briefly, his expression making it clear that he considered it highly unlikely that Violet would win. As he reached for the deck of cards lying in the center of the table, Violet slipped her hand into her reticule.

"Just a moment, Sir Reginald. I brought a fresh deck of cards. I do so hate playing with soiled ones." She smiled pleasantly at him as she placed hers on the table.

"Of course, Lady Danby," he said impassively. Lord Ashby made himself comfortable close to the table where he had an excellent observation post, and he rose periodically to stroll around the table. Sir Reginald doubtless understood the significance of his presence, but neither his expression nor his manner betrayed his dismay. He cast an occasional sidelong glance at Lord Ashby, who continued to study the game intently.

Beyond his instructions to see to it that Sir Reginald played an honest game of piquet, Lord Ashby had no very clear idea of duties. Lady Danby had told him she was relying upon his expertise as a card player to assist her in tonight's game. When she had hinted that Sir Reginald might be guilty of fuzzing the cards, he had been not at all surprised, for he had heard tales of Sir Reginald and recognized him as a Captain Sharp, although he had not heard of his dealings with Evan St. Clair. What he had not expected, however, was that Lady Danby would show herself to be a very proficient card player, shrewd and experienced. He could not be expected to know how many quiet evenings she had passed with Mrs. Crawford, who was herself a virtuoso among piquet players. Despite his misgivings about this evening's entertainment, Ashby found himself fascinated by the game.

At Lady Danby's suggestion, they were playing for pound points. Lord Ashby had attempted to protest, but he had been sharply called to order by both of the interested parties.

"Cocksure, are you not, my lady?" Sir Reginald had inquired. "I hope you may not regret it."

"On the contrary," responded Violet affably, "I am certain that you hope I will regret it very much."

He smiled, acknowledging her home hit. As he had told her during their interview the day before, he found his pockets sadly to let at the moment, and he welcomed the opportunity of lining them so easily. Although he had resorted to less than honest means when he won the diamond brooch from her, he felt quite sure that he would be able to best her honestly with very little trouble. With Lord Ashby hovering so annoyingly close, however, he had no choice but to rely solely upon his own skills.

The game began slowly, each of them studying the other carefully. The first rubber went to Sir Reginald, as did the second, and he was moved to suggest that they play for fifty pounds the rubber as well. Violet, who had held back in her bidding, hoping for just such a suggestion, agreed quietly, ignoring Lord Ashby's horrified expression and whispered protests. Both of them settled in for serious play, and after an hour had passed, Sir Reginald could see that his opponent was moving steadily ahead. Lord Ashby settled himself comfortably in his chair and watched entranced as the game continued. Lady Danby proved to be a formidable player and two hours later Sir Reginald leaned back in his chair, his face flushed, as Lord Ashby gleefully tallied the score.

"You have gone down to the tune of eighteen hundred pounds!" he announced happily to Sir Reginald.

"I fear that I am quite rolled up," said Sir Reginald quietly. "This must end our play, I fear,"

"Perhaps not, Sir Reginald," said Violet coolly. "Have you nothing else you would care to stake? You might come about yet, you know."

"It is possible, Lady Danby, although my luck does not appear to be in tonight. You have held all the cards."

"Luck does change; it is, I believe, a maxim of the game," she replied, taking a sip of champagne.

"You could be right," he answered thoughtfully, mulling the matter over carefully. The chit's luck could not hold forever and she must be growing weary, for the hour was late. If he could come about, his temporary financial embarrassment would be nicely taken care of and he would have had the satisfaction of teaching Lady Danby a much-needed lesson.

"I was thinking, Sir Reginald, that I should very much like to own a pair of diamond eardrops to wear with my brooch," Violet said idly. "Should you have something such as that in your possession, I believe I would agree to any stakes."

The change in Sir Reginald was alarming: his flushed countenance became ashen and he stared at Lady Danby. When he spoke, his lightness of tone was forced, drawing a puzzled glance from Lord Ashby.

"I do not think I have anything like that, Lady Danby. My taste runs more towards rings," he replied.

"And brooches," she reminded him gently. "Perhaps if you will but consider for a moment, you will think of where you could come by such a pair."

"Come now, Sir Reginald," said a gruff voice, "she has you fairly, you know. Surely you can conjure up some eardrops for the lady when I know from personal experience that you have certainly won enough sparklers over the years." The speaker a bluff, red-faced man, laughed heartily at his own words.

Sir Reginald glanced up sharply and saw to his chagrin that a small group had gathered at the edge of the screen of potted palms and had witnessed his losses. If he did not bring himself about now, the news of his loss to this chit of a girl would be all over London by tomorrow morning and it would be long before he could reestablish his credit.

"You have no choice, Sir Reginald, as you see," said Violet in a quiet voice. "We shall begin with the eardrops, if you understand me."

He understood her all too well. He thought of the St. Clair diamonds that were securely locked away in his lodgings. He had had fond hopes of setting up his own gaming establishment soon, somewhere on the Continent. Two, or at the most, three more months would have seen him there. He cursed his luck silently. If only he had decided to wait abroad instead of remaining here in London, he would not now be faced by this brass-faced girl who dared to threaten him. It was with difficulty that he restrained himself from grinding his teeth.

Finally he managed a travesty of a smile and with it a brief, cold bow to Violet. "If you will excuse me, madam, I will send a note round to my man."

She inclined her head graciously. Lord Ashby, most unhappy at the notoriety they were gaining, hurried her away to another quiet corner and brought her a plate of refreshments.

"Must confess, Lady Danby," he said to her admiringly, "thought you was touched in your upper works to play a Captain Sharp like Hawke. Thought you was all about in your head, but you're a regular out-and-outer." It suddenly occurred to him that defeating a gamester on his own ground might not raise Lady Danby in the esteem of some of the starchier members of the ton, so he added hastily, "Of course, must say it still ain't the thing to do. It'll be bellows to mend with me when this gets about."

"You were wonderful to bring me, Lord Ashby," she said warmly. "I shall never forget you for this."

"Daresay I shan't forget it either," he said gloomily. Now that he was no longer absorbed in the game, he had the leisure to again consider his own part in this very questionable outing. Fortunately, Sir Reginald's lodgings were not far distant and his man was efficient, so Lord Ashby's unhappy reflections were not of long duration. Soon they were seating themselves again at the card table and an interested group gathered round them.

Lord Ashby might have decried the attention they were attracting, but Violet was glad of it. With this many pairs of eyes following each move, there would be no opportunity for Sir Reginald to attempt anything havey-cavey. She had greatly feared that his desperation might drive him to it.

In the center of the table lay the pair of diamond eardrops that had been delivered to him. One of the young dandies standing beside her adjusted his quizzing glass and stared at them. "That's a dashed fine pair of sparklers you'll be wearing, Lady Danby," he commented.

"Perhaps she won't be wearing them at all, Cavendish," snarled Sir Reginald, not lifting his eyes from his cards.

"From what I've seen so far, I'd lay a monkey that she will," replied Cavendish cheerfully. A ripple of laughter coursed through the group, causing Sir Reginald to tighten his grip on his cards convulsively, his knuckles growing white.

"I say, Cavendish, button up and let them concentrate on their play," remarked one of his companions, and a silence settled over them as they watched.

The minutes ticked by and Violet continued to move steadily ahead. Her attention was distracted by a sudden, convulsive movement on the part of Lord Ashby. She looked at him questioningly, but his gaze was riveted to the group of onlookers. She glanced up and saw Lord Hartford standing there, his eyes fixed upon the pair of eardrops in the center of the green baize table. As she stared at him, his gaze lifted to her face and she was startled by the blazing anger she saw there. He opened his mouth to speak, but then clamped it shut again.

Violet forced herself to concentrate on her cards and ignore the furious figure that loomed above her. Accordingly, she did not know at what point he walked away. At the end of another hour of play, Violet laid down her last card.

"Piqued, repiqued, and capotted!" exclaimed young Cavendish happily. "You are in the basket, Sir

Reginald."

Violet reached out and picked up the diamonds. "I fancy that you thought I was a pigeon for the plucking, Sir Reginald. Perhaps you will think twice before attempting to bullock me again." As she rose from the table, she turned for one last comment. "I do hope that these are not paste, Sir Reginald," she said sweetly.

Lord Hartford was waiting for them as they left Mrs. Mason's. He bowed to Violet ironically.

"I see that your effrontery knows no bounds, Lady Danby. I had thought that you possessed no other diamonds but the brooch and the ring, but I suppose that you did not feel bound to be truthful in the matter. At least you did not game them away," he said angrily, for fearing to lose them, she had removed her own eardrops and secured the diamonds in place.

"I say, Alistair," began Lord Ashby.

"I will not discuss your part in this before Lady Danby, Ashby. I will call upon you tomorrow morning." And so saying, he stalked away into the darkness.

Thrown into disorder by this attack, Lord Ashby stared after him in dismay. "knew he would be in the deuce of a pucker and fly up into the boughs," he remarked gloomily. "Though why he should think them eardrops was yours, I can't imagine. Perhaps he was rather up in the world."

"It was just his odious way of thinking that he always knows everything. Let him think what he will!"

"All very well for you to say, Lady Danby. He won't call you out."

"He would not do such a thing to you!" gasped Violet.

"Might," replied Lord Ashby. "Perhaps just offer to draw my cork, though," he said more hopefully.

"He cannot be allowed to do such a thing!" exclaimed Violet, horrified. "After all, you were just looking after me."

"*We* know that, but he won't regard it. Plain as a pikestaff that he's taken this very hard, and Alistair is devilish handy with his fives."

"Do not give it another thought, Lord Ashby. I shall take care of this matter," replied Violet grimly. "Odious, detestable man!" she said angrily as she swept into the hall of Granville House.

Not comforted at all by this reassurance, Lord Ashby betook himself home to await the arrival of his guest. The hour was already very late and he fully expected Alistair to be angry enough to arrive at the earliest possible moment the next morning. Sighing, Ashby settled himself comfortably in a chair by the fire with his nightcap on, a brandy by his side.

Chapter Fifteen

Lord Ashby's misgiving proved to be quite accurate, for his man gently shook him awake at an unfashionably early hour the next morning to announce that Lord Hartford had called. Ashby welcomed him uneasily, strategically placing his chair between himself and his caller after taking one look at Alistair's face. His hasty action brought the glimmer of a smile from his friend and Hartford cordially invited him to be seated.

"Not just yet," said Lord Ashby uneasily, measuring the distance to the door with his eye. "Let me explain first."

"By all means," said Lord Hartford amiably, settling himself in a chair to listen. Encouraged by this display of friendliness, Ashby relaxed enough to give a tolerably coherent explanation of the evening at Mrs. Mason's and Lord Hartford listened attentively.

When he had finished, Hartford shook his head slowly. "She should not have been in such a place," he began.

"Knew that! Told her so!" replied Ashby promptly. "Had the bit between her teeth and wouldn't listen."

Hartford held up his hands. "I believe you, Ash. I know what she's like when she is determined to do something. No, I acquit you of any responsibility in the matter. You did the only thing possible by escorting her."

Relieved by his response, Lord Ashby emerged from his strategic position and seated himself. "Game as a pebble," he commented. "Pluck to the backbone. Never blinked an eye while she was playing him."

"Yes, very true," Hartford responded. He stared into the fire for a moment. "But you say that Sir Reginald had those diamond eardrops, Ash, not Lady Danby?"

"She had them at the end of the evening because she won them, but Sir Reginald had them to begin with."

Lord Hartford's eyes were shining. "Extraordinary!" he murmured.

"I don't know that," argued Ashby knowledgeably. "Don't say they weren't a pretty pair of sparklers because they were, but not extraordinary. In fact," he said thoughtfully, "seems to me that I've seen a pair just like them before."

Lord Hartford stared at him in amusement. "Of course you have, you gudgeon. I know that you will not mention this to anyone, Ash, so I tell you in confidence." Ashby nodded to assure his friend of his silence and Hartford continued. "They are the eardrops that belong to the St. Clair diamonds.

You have seen my aunt wear them."

"Dash it all, Alistair, what was Sir Reginald doing with part of the St. Clair diamonds? And, come to think of it, how did Lady Danby know he had 'em? She did, you know, told him as pretty as you please that she wanted to play for a pair of eardrops to go with that brooch of hers."

"I see," answered Alistair thoughtfully. "Yes, I should very much like to know the answer to both those questions, Ashby. I think I shall make it my business to find out."

He set out immediately for Granville House to call on Violet, but discovered upon his arrival there that she had left in haste a few minutes earlier. Balked of his prey, Lord Hartford decided to pay a call on Sir Reginald Hawke instead.

The morning was not destined to be a pleasant one for Sir Reginald. He had awakened at an unseasonably early hour with a shocking headache, having indulged in the better part of three bottles of excellent Burgundy after suffering his indignity at the hands of Lady Danby the night before. Indeed, the jokes and slighting remarks he had been subjected to at Mrs. Mason's before he could depart had wounded him to the quick and he bore them no better in the full light of day.

Having just drifted back into an uneasy half-slumber, he was understandably annoyed to hear his man reenter his room. When he demanded to know why he had been awakened, his valet, a small, dark man who had been in his service for many years and was privy to all of his secrets, had given him a note from Lady Danby, which he read with glazed eyes. It informed him that she was aware that he had possession of the St. Clair necklace and bracelet and very likely the real brooch and ring as well, assuming that hers were indeed made of paste. She assured him that she could wait until tomorrow to act upon her knowledge, but at that time she could see that her duty required her to share that knowledge with Lord Granville, the dowager countess, and Lord Hartford. She anxiously awaited his reply.

Sir Reginald knew that he was in a most unenviable position. He could deny possession of the jewels, of course, or assert that he had won them in play, which indeed he had, however unfairly, but he was certain that once Lord Hartford became involved in the matter, things would become damnably unpleasant. He held his head in his hands, wishing that he had not indulged in that third bottle of Burgundy. If only his present business affairs were settled, he would have enough money to leave the country and begin afresh in some other land less familiar with his particular talents. Cursing, he had laid the note down and tried to think.

Being singularly unsuccessful in that undertaking, he had required his man to bring him a beefsteak and ale to recruit his strength, and he was thus employed when Lord Hartford was announced. Before he could deny his presence, his unwelcome visitor had entered the room and stood looking down at him. Sir Reginald knew himself to be at a distinct disadvantage, seated as he was in his dressing gown behind his breakfast, and with an attempt at cordiality, invited Lord Hartford to be seated.

"Thank you, but I prefer to stand," was the

160

daunting response. "My business will not take long. I would like to know, Sir Reginald, how those diamond eardrops that you lost to Lady Danby last night came into your possession."

Sir Reginald allowed himself the ghost of a smile, a liberty that he immediately regretted as he noted Hartford's expression.

"I fear that it would not be the part of a gentleman to make that known to you, Hartford," he responded gently.

"That should present no problem for you, Sir Reginald," was the brusque response.

Sir Reginald's face darkened in anger at the insult, but, knowing that Lord Hartford was an excellent shot, he managed to bite back the stinging retort that sprang to his lips. With an attempt at ease, he said, "Now, Hartford, we are, after all, men of the world. It should come as no shock to you if I won them in gaming."

"No, I had thought as much, knowing your reputation. But from whom did you win them?"

Sir Reginald's only response was a slightly lifted eyebrow. Seeing that Lord Hartford still waited grimly for a response, he shrugged lightly and said, "From whom would you think, sir?"

Lord Hartford stared at him furiously and his hands clenched involuntarily. Sir Reginald took note of this and was grateful when his guest satisfied himself with a stiff bow and took himself silently from the room.

With a small, satisfied smile, Sir Reginald leaned back in his chair. "Let us see how you handle that one, my pretty," he thought viciously, thinking of

Lady Danby.

The subject of his malice was far too busy at that particular moment to spare a thought for the St. Clair diamonds. Early that morning she had received an urgent note from Lady Sally, asking her to come to Hill Street as soon as humanly possible. It was obvious from Sally's scrawl that the note had been written in haste and while she was suffering some emotional disturbance. Violet had dressed hurriedly, dismissed Summers, and summoned the carriage.

Lady Sally was watching for her anxiously from the drawing-room window and met her at the door, to the obvious disapproval of the butler. She shepherded Violet into the drawing room and closed the doors securely.

"Penelope," she said in a low voice, pulling her friend onto the sofa beside her, "you have stood my friend thus far and kept my confidences. Can you continue to do so?" Her eyes looked feverish and Violet wondered for a moment if she were ill.

She nodded her head slowly. "I will at least do what I can to help you, Sally. What is it? What has happened?"

"The most wonderful thing imaginable, Penelope!" exclaimed Sally. "I am in love!"

Violet looked somewhat daunted by this bit of news. "Yes, I know, Sally. I realize that you were married to Lord Randolph last spring."

"Don't be such a ninnyhammer, Penelope. It isn't John of whom I am speaking. It is Sir Geoffrey."

"Sir Geoffrey? But what of your husband, Sally?" asked Violet, looking stunned.

"Pray, what has John to say to anything? He is hundreds of miles away and he chose to go without me," replied Lady Sally petulantly.

"You told me that Lord Randolph had no choice but to go and that he would not allow you to make such a long, arduous journey because he feared for your health."

"Rubbish! If he cared a fig for me, he would not have gone at all. Geoffrey says that he would never leave me in such a cold-hearted way."

"Fortunately for Sir Geoffrey, he has not been called upon to prove that," retorted Violet, taking up the cudgels on behalf of the absent Lord Randolph.

"Had I known that you would take this . . . this *Methodist* outlook, I would not have confided in you," said Lady Sally stiffly.

Violet suddenly wondered what else her friend had planned to tell her and she realized with misgiving that shatterbrained Sally might be talking of more than simply taking a lover.

"I am sorry to pinch at you, Sally," she said, forcing herself to apologize. "I would be glad to see you happy." Violet reflected that she did indeed wish for Sally's happiness, and she considered it highly unlikely that Sir Geoffrey would provide it.

"I knew that you would be!" she exclaimed. "Now you sound more like yourself! And I simply *had* to tell someone, Penelope, before I burst."

"Just what are you telling me, Sally? I don't think I quite understand?"

Lady Sally became suddenly shy. "I won't be alone any longer, Penelope," she said softly. "Geof-

163

frey has promised me that he will never leave me."

"Never leave you?" asked Violet, startled.

"We are eloping, Penelope, and I need your help. He will call for me this afternoon, and I would like for you to be here with me so that it appears we are all setting out for an afternoon expedition. We will set you down when we get a few blocks away, and Geoffrey and I will drive on to his home in Kent. It will be several hours before anyone realizes that we are gone, and Alistair will not be able to overtake us. Will you do it?" she asked pleadingly.

Violet's mind was racing. She could not allow Lady Sally to throw away her reputation and her happiness for Sir Geoffrey. She was quite certain that he did not at all love Sally and equally certain from what Sally had told her that Lord Randolph did. Lady Sally, young and heedless, had become bored and fancied herself in love. Violet had noticed Sir Geoffrey at Mrs. Mason's last night, and he had not been alone. He had had a handsome redhead on his arm and he had disappeared as soon as he realized that Lady Danby was present. Violet shook her head. It was a despicable thing to do, but she decided that she must betray her friend for her own good.

Accordingly, Violet smiled at Lady Sally. "Of course I will help you," she replied. She left her friend happily making plans and returned to Granville House, where she found Lord Hartford awaiting her.

Before he had an opportunity to question her about her gaming with Sir Reginald, she said absently, stripping off her gloves, "Pray be seated, sir.

Have you any plans for this afternoon?"

His eyes widened at the unexpected question. "No, but I am not here to discuss my schedule," he replied briefly, preparing to launch into his interrogation.

"Excellent! For I shall need for you be at Lady Sally's home promptly at two o'clock."

"At Sally's? Whatever for?" he asked, momentarily distracted.

"To prevent an elopement," she said quietly.

"Elopement? Who is eloping?" he asked in disbelief.

"Your sister and Sir Geoffrey Hayes."

"Impossible!" he replied angrily. "Sally would do nothing so improper!"

"Would she not?" Violet asked drily.

"She would never abandon her husband and her position. Such an act would ruin her. She would not be such a fool!"

"Then you have more confidence in her than I, Lord Hartford. She fancies herself neglected and is ripe for any folly. Sir Geoffrey is not a man to overlook such an opportunity."

"How would you know?" he asked her directly.

Violet flushed. "He is not a man of principle," she replied slowly. "He spends his time with men such as Sir Reginald, for one thing. And if he is indeed so besotted by Sally, why was he at Mrs. Mason's last night with another woman? He does not think that I saw him, but I did. I am not sure what his purpose is in eloping with Sally, whether he is doing it as a lark or whether he has a darker reason, perhaps blackmailing her or her family."

165

She looked at him directly. "I know what you think of me, Lord Hartford, but I do assure you that I could not allow your sister to ruin herself and only stand by and watch it happen. I do not like to betray her. She trusts me to keep my word, for I have always done so. But I could not allow her to do this."

Lord Hartford looked at her searchingly. "If what you say is true, I shall be greatly in your debt, Lady Danby, and I shall be most grateful."

"Your sister will not be grateful. I fear that I may well lose my friend."

"Only temporarily, I am sure. She will come to her senses in time and then she too will thank you."

"I hope that I am still alive to hear it," commented Violet drily.

She explained their plans to him, and both deciding that he would pay an unexpected call on Lady Sally just after Violet arrived there and he would remain for the entire afternoon, thus foiling their elopement for the moment. They were also determined to expose Sir Geoffrey's perfidy to Sally so that she would no longer be tempted to fly with him. After a few moments of thought, Violet dispatched a note to Lord Ashby, describing the woman she had seen with Sir Geoffrey at Mrs. Mason's, and asking him to discover her identity as quickly as possible.

Lord Hartford watched grimly as she handed the note to a footman to deliver. "I see that you and Ashby are wondrous close," he commented drily. "You seem to take it for granted that he will do as you ask immediately."

Violet looked surprised. "Yes, of course," she answered. "He is all that is obliging."

Lord Ashby was startled by her request, but took it in good part, and immediately set about finding the name of Sir Geoffrey's lady. A few inquiries innocently made at his club elicited the name of Maria Davenport, better known as the Dasher. Ashby hesitated briefly over the propriety of speaking of such a notable Cyprian to a gently bred female, but Violet made short work of his reservations.

"That is wonderful, Lord Ashby," she said gratefully. "And you have got her direction, too. I cannot thank you enough."

Lord Ashby looked gratified, but still puzzled. "Can't think why you should want to know," he commented. "Ain't the thing at all. Dash it all, don't go telling Alistair about it."

"Oh, he already knows, and he is quite as grateful as I am."

"Is he indeed?" asked Lord Ashby, staggered. He was still shaking his head as he departed from Granville House. Things had come to a pretty pass when Alistair Fitzhugh discussed famous Cyprians with his cousin's widow.

Violet penned a careful note to the Dasher, inviting her to meet Sir Geoffrey in front of Mrs. Mason's just at eight o'clock that evening, and another to be delivered to Sir Geoffrey's lodgings later that afternoon, telling him that the Dasher would be delighted to spend the evening with him if he would meet her at eight o'clock in front of Mrs. Mason's establishment. Satisfied with her morning's work, Violet put away her pen and went upstairs to prepare for that afternoon.

Everything worked according to plan. Lord Hartford arrived in Hill Street in time to prevent their driving away. With widened eyes, Sally sat in the drawing room with her guests as Lord Hartford chatted idly, regaling them with the latest *on-dits*. When Sir Geoffrey was finally forced to leave, Lord Hartford suggested a play at Covent Garden that evening, virtually forcing his sister to accept. Exhausted, Lady Sally watched him depart.

"I cannot believe it, Penelope. Alistair *never* calls on me in the afternoon and he certainly never stays this long." She collapsed onto the sofa and sighed. "Now we cannot possibly leave until tomorrow."

She seized Violet's hand as she rose to leave. "Thank you for coming, Penelope," she said gratefully.

Feeling like a traitor, Violet finally made her escape, telling herself that this was for Sally's own good. She hardened her heart as she thought of Lord Hartford and Sally stopping in front of Mrs. Mason's just long enough for her to see Sir Geoffrey with his inamorata. The pain of discovering his infidelity would be as nothing compared with the pain Sally would feel if she abandoned her marriage.

Relieved that Lord Hartford would be faced with that portion of the plan, Violet prepared herself for dinner. After rereading a new letter from Penelope that she had been carrying in her reticule, she opened the dressing-table drawer and pulled out her packet of letters from home. Frowning, she saw that the blue ribbon which had bound them together lay loose in the bottom of the drawer. That was strange, she reflected, for she always tied them neatly together.

Shrugging, she tied them together again and closed the drawer. Now she would see what she could do about clearing Penelope of any connection with the diamonds. Summers snuffed out the candles and Violet walked slowly downstairs to face her ordeal with the dowager.

Chapter Sixteen

Penelope stood in the brilliant autumn sunlight, watching Evan playing at the bottom of the garden, where the gardener's assistant was working in the flower beds. He had become extremely fond of the new gardener, a strong, open-faced young man, and stayed as close as possible to Jem when he could find him. Penelope had been a little uneasy at first since he was a newcomer to the district and they knew little of him, but Bartlett, Mrs. Crawford's elderly, crotchety gardener, said that he was smart and reliable and knew his flowers. High praise indeed from one inclined to be suspicious and regard anyone new as an interloper. They had all become accustomed to Jem's quiet presence in their small household and Penelope, Mrs. Crawford, and Peters, Evan's nanny, were all inclined to relax while Evan was with him.

Knowing that she did not need to watch him so closely now, Penelope allowed her mind to wander and she gave herself up to the luxury of worrying about Violet. Her letters were always newsy, telling of the many parties and balls she attended, but very little was said about Violet herself. Penelope thought that she could read between the lines and that her sister was deeply worried about something. Her last two letters had sounded strangely strained and unlike her cheerful, chatty sister. It required no stretching of the imagination to believe that Violet had gotten herself into some predicament. The only question was which sort of predicament it was. It made Penelope uneasy to think of Violet so far away with no one to turn to if she were in trouble.

Violet's description of the St. Clair family had made it quite clear that no help would be forthcoming from any of them, with the possible exception of Lady Dora. Unfortunately, she did not possess either power or money, so it was doubtful that she could be of any particular assistance. Her sister's graphic descriptions of the dowager had made Penelope shudder and be devoutly grateful that she had refused to go herself. The mere thought that such a dragon might have control of her son was more than she could bear thinking of. It was true that she had given Violet an allowance and helped her to be recognized socially, but Penelope was worldly enough to realize that these things had been done more as a matter of pride than from any wish to be kind.

Penelope drifted slowly down toward the river, idly watching the leaves floating on its azure surface as she puzzled over her problem. Her hand went to the pocket of her gown, and she drew out the silver snuffbox that Violet had sent and rubbed her hand over its shining surface. So long ago it all seemed now. She could still picture Evan's bright, loving countenance though. The few letters she had had time to receive from him before his death were kept carefully on her dressing table in a carved box which contained the few small mementos she had of their brief marriage. She looked down at her hands, unadorned by jewelry. The only ring she ever wore was the diamond one she had sent with Violet. It seemed strange that you could miss an inanimate thing so much. Without it Evan seemed even farther away, so she carried the snuffbox instead.

So absorbed was she in her thoughts that she failed to notice the dark carriage that rolled quietly into the lane that ran along the west edge of Mrs. Crawford's property, nor did Jem, his head bent close to his work, hear its approach. The only person who seemed at all interested was Evan, and he began toddling straight for the boundary of the property. The carriage paused in the shadow of a hawthorn hedge, its driver, a small, dark man wrapped in a driving coat with his hat pulled low over his eyes, watched as the boy stopped, fascinated. The carriage door opened and a rather heavyset man descended, a stick of peppermint held invitingly in his outstretched hand. Evan recognized the treat and smiled, walking closer to the road. There was a sudden flurry of activity and a small cry from Evan as the heavyset man swept him into the carriage and the driver cracked the whip to move the horses away at a spanking clip.

Both Penelope and Jem looked up at the sound. Penelope screamed and ran toward the road, but Jem, dropping his tools along the way, passed her easily and stared after the rapidly disappearing carriage. Without a word to Penelope, he ran back to the stable, saddled a horse, and galloped down the road after them. Mrs. Crawford and some of the house servants found Penelope crying hysterically in the middle of the road and it took some time before her aunt could wrest from her the story of what had happened. A puzzled groom had reported to her that the new assistant gardener had saddled a horse and ridden it away without as much as a by-your-leave, and Mrs. Crawford sent him straightaway to report the kidnapping to the magistrate in Bath.

As Mrs. Crawford was fond of saying later, she didn't know whether she was on her head or her heels for the rest of the day and through that night, what with people coming and going and asking questions about Evan and the carriage and Jem, who had not returned. She had had the presence of mind, after putting Penelope to bed with a few laudanum drops and Emma to look after her, to send a letter to Violet, telling her of the kidnapping and asking her to come home to them immediately. This she had given to the groom and instructed him not to linger along the way.

On that same autumn evening, Violet was involved in momentous affairs herself. Determined to clear up the matter of the diamonds, she steeled herself to talk with the dowager after dinner, who somewhat ungraciously agreed to speak with her. Lady Dora gathered up her needlework to leave the room, but Violet held out her hand to her and smiled.

"Pray, do stay, Lady Dora. What I am going to tell Lady Granville concerns you as well."

Lady Dora resumed her seat and glanced uneasily at her sister, who cleared her throat loudly and struck the floor with her cane.

"Well, girl, what do you wish to speak to me about? Come to the point quickly."

Violet ignored her brusque tone and quietly began her tale, careful to omit any mention of Evan or Penelope.

"I wish to speak to you, madam, concerning the St. Clair diamonds."

The dowager struck the floor again and uttered a triumphant croak. "Hah!" she said loudly, turning to her sister. "I told you she had 'em, but you would not believe me, nor would Alistair. Now we'll get to the bottom of the matter. Speak up quickly, girl. Where are they?"

Violet, struck by the allusion to Hartford, ignored her command. "Lord Hartford did not believe that I had the diamonds?" she asked incredulously.

"Nor did he, the more fool he! I warned him that a pretty face was a man's undoing. Fancy his being taken in just like my Evan when he considers himself awake on every suit."

"You are mistaken, Lady Granville," Violet said frostily. "I did not take the diamonds."

"Nonsense, my girl, where would they be if you did not? And you just said that you were going to tell us about them."

"And so I am, Your Ladyship, if you will allow me to do it in my own way."

The dowager muttered audibly about upstarts and mushrooms, but Lady Dora quieted her and nodded encouragingly to Violet. "Go ahead, my dear. I am eager to hear it."

"When we were married, Evan presented me with the ring and the brooch that I have worn so often here. He told me that they were family heirlooms and that his mother had sent them to him for his bride."

The dowager snorted loudly at this and Violet flushed, but, remembering Penelope, she held her head high and continued. "Yes, I know what you think, Lady Granville, but indeed he did tell me that. He said that his cousin, Bevil St. Clair, had followed him the night of his quarrel with you and his father and that Mr. St. Clair had told him that you sent him these pieces secretly. Evan believed that you, at least, had relented and it made him happy."

Lady Granville opened her mouth to speak, but Violet held up her hand. "Pray let me continue, Lady Granville. I know now that you did not send those pieces, for I asked Lord Granville, and he assured me that Evan's account was not accurate. He told me that he followed Evan to offer any help that he could, but that he certainly had not given him the ring and the brooch."

There was a brief silence while the two older ladies stared at her. Violet continued, a little hesitantly. "I could not think why Evan would have told me something that was not true," she said slowly.

The dowager interrupted her brusquely. "My son would not have told you something that was not true. He was a man of honor. You are the one not speaking the truth."

Violet colored, but said quietly enough, "Indeed, I assure you, madam, that I am telling the truth as I know it. I find it curious that you would believe that your son took the diamonds and yet you would say that he would not lie and that he was a man of honor. The two are contradictory."

It was Lady Granville's turn to flush, a deep,

unbecoming red. "I never believed that my son was responsible for the loss of the diamonds. It appeared to be his fault," she said, her voice becoming the querulous, quavering voice of a much older woman, "but he would never have done such a thing had you not encouraged him."

"But I assure you that I did not do so," said Violet quietly, "and it appears to me that there may be another explanation, although I fear that you will like it even less than your present one."

Quickly she told them of losing the butterfly brooch to Sir Reginald and his assertion that the piece was paste. Glancing apologetically at the dowager, she said that she had discovered that shortly before his marriage Evan had lost a great deal of money while gambling with Sir Reginald.

"And if he did, what of it?" demanded the dowager. "That was no more than a young man sowing his wild oats, as I told his father. It was his bad luck that he fell into the hands of a Captain Sharp like Hawke, but my husband would not listen. He sent Evan away and look what came of it," she said bitterly.

"Had it occurred to you, Lady Granville, that Evan might have lost more than you or your husband knew about?" asked Violet. "That he might have lost the diamonds in play and replaced them with paste replicas?"

The dowager rose unsteadily to her feet. "I will hear no more of this!" she said imperiously. "You are trying to blame my son for your own misdeeds when he cannot defend himself! I tell you that Evan St. Clair would never have done such a despicable thing. If you can believe this of him, then you never knew my son nor loved him."

"But Lady Granville, I have the diamond eardrops from the set." She held them out for her to see. "I won these in play from Sir Reginald and I am certain that he has the other jewels in his possession. How else would he have come by them if Evan did not lose them to him while gaming?"

Lady Granville sat down heavily in her chair, her face drained of color. Indeed she looked so ill that Violet ran for the smelling salts and Lady Dora chafed her wrists worriedly. Lady Granville waved them both away and sat up stiffly.

"I cannot believe this, but we shall certainly get to the bottom of it. Dora, send a note round to Alistair at once and ask him to call as soon as possible."

Lady Dora hurried away to comply with her command, and Lady Granville turned abruptly in her chair to stare at Violet.

"This is not true, you know. I can see that you do believe it, however." Her eyes glittered dangerously. "How can you say that you loved my son and in the same breath accuse him of being little better than a common thief?"

Violet, thinking of Penelope and her unquestioning faith in Evan, had the grace to blush. She murmured something incoherent and fled to the haven of her bedroom, wishing that the whole ugly business were over with. How could she ever face her sister after exposing the dishonor of her husband? It had been hard enough to face Evan's mother. At least she had the comfort of knowing that Alistair would not be calling that evening, for his business with Lady Sally would require all of his attention.

Chapter Seventeen

Breakfast the next morning was a silent affair. The dowager maintained a haughty silence and Violet had no heart for talking herself. Only poor Lady Dora made spasmodic attempts to act as though there were nothing wrong, and finally even she abandoned the effort and lapsed into a gloomy silence. Nor did things brighten when Lady Sally put in an early appearance. Her face was pale and deep blue crescents beneath her eyes told of her sleepless night. She directed a speaking glance to Violet and the two retired to the morning room.

Once there, Sally forgot all attempts at formality and burst into tears.

"He is a traitor, Penelope, a black-hearted scoundrel. On the very night that we were to have eloped, Geoffrey was entertaining another . . . lady!" She spat the last word out with an effort. "She was no real lady, however, but a very striking Cyprian. Much more dashing than I shall ever be," she added disconsolately.

"Nonsense!" said Violet bracingly. "You have broken more hearts than any lightskirt Sir Geoffrey may have taken up with. Everyone knows that you are a diamond of the first water. Think of how many men were cast into despair when you married Lord Randolph."

Lady Sally brightened considerably. "Yes, that is true," she admitted. "Oh, I know that you are roasting me, Penelope, but it does help. I am not such a mean bit, after all, am I?"

Seeing that only her friend's vanity had been wounded and not her heart, Violet laughed. "Goose! How can you even say such a thing? Think of the gentlemen who will be lining up to take Sir Geoffrey's place."

"I shall be much more selective this time," Lady Sally frowned. "I wonder whether Lord Elton or Sir Lloyd would be best?"

Encouraged by Sally's choices, one a staid but elegant middle-aged bachelor and the other little more than a halfling, although an engaging one, Violet fell into a discussion of their relative merits. The time passed quickly and the two were startled when Lord Ashby suddenly erupted into the room without being announced. Ruffing closed the door behind him, obviously outraged by this flagrant breach of good manners.

Lady Sally, too, looked affronted. "Honestly, Ash, of all the rag-mannered—"

"Beg pardon, I'm sure," wheezed Lord Ashby, lowering himself breathlessly into a chair. "An emergency, or I wouldn't have, I assure you," he began, but broke off, catching Violet's eye.

"The thing is, Lady Sally," he said apologetically, "I must speak to Lady Danby privately."

Lady Sally looked from one to the other and then rose to her feet, the picture of wounded dignity. "I see," she said frigidly. "Not for the world would I intrude where I am not wanted."

"Oh, I am sorry, Sally," apologized Violet. "Lord Ashby was kind enough to take care of a small business matter for me, and I must speak to him for a few moments. Please let Ruffing show you to the drawing room to wait. I shall be just a minute."

Lady Sally shook her head stubbornly. "Certainly not. Not for the world would I intrude," she repeated in a martyred tone. "Although I never would have believed that you would be setting up a flirt, Ashby," she said maliciously.

Before the maligned Lord Ashby could retort, Lady Sally had swept majestically from the room, damaging the effect of her exit a trifle when she caught the hem of her skirt in the door and had to open it to extract it.

"She is the most exasperating girl!" exclaimed Violet as the door closed a second time with a bang.

Lord Ashby nodded. "Always has been. Fancy her thinking that we were an item."

"She was only being provoking," said Violet comfortingly. "She must know we are no such thing. But do tell me, Lord Ashby, what has happened."

"Had a note from that fellow Hawke this morning," he replied, drawing a letter from his waistcoat pocket. "Damned cheek of the fellow! Wants to know what it would be worth to me to scotch a story about you. Says that it would be unfortunate if everyone came to hear that Lady Danby had lost the St. Clair diamonds to him in play."

"Blackmail again!" gasped Violet. "But he could not prove such a thing."

"Wouldn't need to," said Lord Ashby bluntly. "Just a whisper here and there and the whole ton would know it. Damage would be done."

"That horrible man!" raged Violet. "He is lower than a . . . than a snake!"

Her companion nodded his agreement. "Not the thing at all. Shocking bad ton. Still, we was seen in his company and you were playing piquet with him. Who's to believe it didn't happen more than once or twice?"

"But there must be something we can do!" she exclaimed, pressing her hands to her forehead. Suddenly she looked up at Lord Ashby. "Whyever did Sir Reginald send that note to you?"

Lord Ashby's face put his cherry-striped waistcoat to shame. "Must think, you know, that we are a twosome. Thought I would be the one to approach."

Violet's eyes widened. "You mean because you were my escort the other evening and because you rescued me from him the first time?"

Lord Ashby nodded unhappily. "Logical thing, I'm afraid. Probably not the only one that thinks it."

Violet was contrite. "Oh, I am so sorry, Lord Ashby, to place you in such an uncomfortable position! And after you have been so very kind."

"Happy to," he said hurriedly. "Thing is, we must decide how to deal with him now. I'm not a cheese-paring fellow as a rule, but it goes against the grain to throw the ready away to a Queer Nabs like Hawke."

"No, we will not pay him anything," said Violet with certainty. She sank into her chair, her chin in her hands. "But we must determine the best thing to do." There was a minute or two of silence while Ashby watched her hopefully.

Ruffing opened the door and entered, looking his most stately to protest Lady Danby's unseemly conduct in entertaining a gentleman alone.

"I beg your pardon, Lady Danby," he said, bowing, "but you have received an urgent message from Stanhope Cottage and I took the liberty of disturbing you."

"Yes, you were quite right to do so. Thank you, Ruffing." She fairly snatched the letter from the tray and ripped it open as Ruffing removed his offended dignity from the room. Scanning its contents impatiently, Violet collapsed into her chair, the color drained from her face.

Lord Ashby watched her nervously. "Someone ill, Lady Danby?" he asked. When she did not reply, he stood. "Mustn't get in your way if there's a problem. Happy to help you if I could."

His voice brought Violet to her feet in a rush.

"Oh, yes, yes indeed, Lord Ashby. It is so kind of you to offer. I do indeed need your help. Could you drive me to Bath?"

Thrown into disorder by this sudden request, he managed to stammer, "Bath? Need to drink the waters?"

"No, no," she replied impatiently. "I need for you to take me home to Stanhope Cottage. My nephew has been kidnapped and I must go to my sister at once."

"Kidnapped?" he asked, shocked. "Nasty business, that!" Recovering himself, he added, "Glad to be of service, of course. I'll just go round and have my bays put to. Be back directly."

"Oh, thank you, Lord Ashby," she exclaimed, showing signs of bursting into tears. "You are very kind." And rushing from the room, she hurried upstairs to throw some things haphazardly into a bandbox. Summers was horrified to discover that Lady Danby had no intention of taking her and pointed out to her that she would be ill-advised to take a long carriage ride unchaperoned, but her mistress ignored her protests. Violet was fully alive to the impropriety of her actions, but she could not take Summers and have her discover that Penelope was really Lady Danby, so she left her abigail in a state of shock. After dashing off a note to her aunts, Violet hurried downstairs to wait anxiously for Lord Ashby.

He was as good as his word and she had not long to wait. Not one hour after the letter arrived at Granville House, Lord Hartford was startled to see his friend's carriage dashing out of the square at a spanking clip and still more startled to see Lady Danby seated with him inside. Lord Ashby threw Hartford an apologetic glance and ducked out of sight, miserably aware that Violet had brought no abigail and that he would undoubtedly soon be having another most uncomfortable chat with his friend about Lady Danby's unconventional behavior.

His aunts were considerably startled when Lord Hartford burst in upon them a few minutes later.

"Alistair!" exclaimed the dowager, awakened from a brief nap by his hasty entrance. "I do wish that you would allow Ruffing to announce you. Not that I am not glad to see you, for we have a great deal to discuss."

"Where has Lady Danby gone?" he asked abruptly, as though his aunt had not spoken.

"How should I know that, Alistair?" replied Lady Granville crossly. "I do not keep track of her every movement. Now . . ."

"I saw her leaving in a carriage with Lord Ashby just a few minutes ago. They were in a great hurry and I would like to know their destination."

"Well, really, Alistair. One would think that she was a person of some consequence to listen to you. I see that we shall get nothing done until you find out, however." Resigned, she rang the bell. "Perhaps Ruffing or Summers can tell us."

Ruffing entered immediately, bearing a note in his hand, and bowed to Lady Granville.

"Ruffing, do you know where Lady Danby went just now?"

"I apprehend, Your Ladyship, that she and Lord Ashby were on their way to Bath," he answered calmly.

"Bath?" Three startled faces turned toward him. "Whatever makes you think that, Ruffing?" inquired his mistress.

"I happened to overhear a comment Lord Ashby made to Lady Danby." He coughed discreetly. "Lady Danby did not think it necessary to take Summers with her, however. She appeared to be quite distraught."

"Did not take Summers with her?" asked the dowager, scandalized. "What could she have been thinking of?"

Ruffing coughed again. "She left Your Ladyship a note." He proffered the letter to Lady Granville, but Lord Hartford intercepted it and ripped it open.

"Alistair! That is addressed to me!"

"I realize that, Aunt, but I assure you that it concerns me as well," he replied, hastily scanning its contents. "There has been an emergency at home. That is all that she says, and that she will send for her things presently."

"A likely tale!" exclaimed Lady Granville. Then, remembering Ruffing's presence, she dismissed him with a nod. "She has gone home to avoid any further discussion of the diamonds, Alistair!"

"Nonsense!" was his brisk reply. "I have been expecting something like this," he said, nodding to the note. "I must follow them immediately. I will be in touch with you as soon as I return to London."

Lady Granville began to protest more forcibly, but she was too late. The door had already closed behind him and Lord Hartford was on his way home to prepare for a trip to Bath.

The dowager and Lady Dora stared at one another in mystified silence, then Lady Granville struck the floor with her cane.

"Ruffing!" she called imperiously. "Order up the carriage and tell my woman to pack my things! I am going to Bath!" She turned to her sister. "I intend to get to the bottom of this matter, Dora."

"Well, you won't do it alone, Maria," she retorted. "I shall accompany you."

Chapter Eighteen

Lord Ashby's carriage was well sprung and his coachman a superior driver; nonetheless, Violet was bone-weary by the time they were set down at Stanhope Cottage. Her aunt's note had been brief, no more than an almost incoherent scrawl announcing that Evan had been kidnapped and asking her to come home. She had searched through her reticule during the journey, looking for the note so that she could reread it, and was disappointed to find that she must have left it in the morning room. Her conversation with Lord Ashby had been no more than desultory, although she had tried to explain a little about the situation he would find at Stanhope Cottage. He knew of course that she had a sister; she had told him that soon after first meeting him. She now informed him that her sister was also a widow and had but the one son.

"What! Both of you widows?" he had asked, shocked. "An extraordinary thing!" If he thought it odd that she had not before mentioned this circumstance or the existence of her nephew, he had too much delicacy to mention it, and consoled himself by ordering refreshments brought out quickly to the coach at every posting-house where they stopped to change cattle.

When the carriage finally stopped in front of the cottage, every light in the house was blazing brightly and the front door opened quickly, spilling a sea of golden light across the travelers. Penelope stood there, her arms outstretched to her sister, her bright hair a shining aureole in the lamplight. For a brief, dazed moment, Lord Ashby thought that he was gazing upon a heavenly vision, but then the vision spoke and threw herself into Lady Danby's arms.

"Oh, dear sister, I am so glad that you are home again!" She buried her face in Violet's shoulder and Violet gently stroked her hair.

"Have you heard anything else, Penny?" Violet asked softly. An incoherent sob was her only reply.

Mrs. Crawford bustled out the door and embraced her niece. "Come in out of the chill, my dears, or you'll catch your deaths." As she gathered them into the tiled entry hall, she looked at Lord Ashby and smiled wearily, holding out her hand. "I do not know you, sir, but you have my gratitude for bringing my niece home to us."

Lord Ashby, tearing his gaze from Penelope's lovely, tear-stained face with some difficulty, smiled at Mrs. Crawford in a bemused manner and absently took her hand.

Violet, reminded of her duties, looked apologetically at him. "I am so sorry, Lord Ashby, to be so rag-mannered, but I quite forgot everything when I saw my sister."

"Quite all right, Lady Danby. Understand it perfectly, in fact. Everything went out of my head when I saw her, too." To his horror, Lord Ashby realized that he was blushing.

"This is Lord Ashby, my most kind friend, Aunt Serena. I have written to you about him. Lord Ashby, this is my aunt, Serena Crawford."

Lord Ashby murmured the proper greetings and Mrs. Crawford thanked him again for his kindness in bringing Violet to them so quickly.

Then, her arms still around Penelope, Violet said hesitantly, "I shall try to explain it to you later, Lord Ashby, and I know that you will find it a trifle confusing at first, but I should like for you to meet my sister, Lady Danby."

Penelope threw her a reproachful glance, and Violet reassured her. "No, no Penny. He will not give you away. You may trust Lord Ashby."

"Indeed you may," Lord Ashby assured her earnestly, his eyes never leaving Penelope's face. "Don't quite understand it, though. Lady Danby, did you say? But I thought—"

"Yes, I know, Lord Ashby, but I am Violet Carlton. It is Penelope who was married to Evan St. Clair and it is their son who is missing."

At the mention of her son, Penelope collapsed again, her shoulders heaving. "We shall never find him, Violet. He has already been gone more than a day and we have had no word of him."

Lord Ashby, distressed by her weeping, stirred uneasily. "How did someone come to take the boy?" he asked.

"Yes, Penny, please stop crying and tell us exactly what happened and what has been done thus far to find Evan."

"It was all my fault, Vi," said Penelope miserably, wringing her handkerchief. "I was not watching as I should have been and I did not see the carriage in the lane. Then I heard the sound of a scuffle and Evan crying out and the carriage drove away very quickly." She put her hands to her face. "I would have been watching him more carefully, but I thought that he was with Jem."

"Who is Jem?" asked Violet sharply.

"The new gardener's assistant," replied her aunt promptly. "A very likely young man we all thought and very fond of the boy. We had no reason to think anything but good of him until this."

"Where is he now?" asked Violet. "I should like to talk to him."

"So should we all," said Mrs. Crawford unhappily, "but he jumped on one of our horses and rode away after the carriage before anyone could stop him."

"So he was a part of it," mused Violet. "It must have been planned then, Aunt, very carefully. It seems strange that you have not heard anything from the kidnappers. One would think that they would ask for a ransom. Why take Evan if not for money?"

Her aunt's kindly face crumpled. "That's what we don't know, my dear. And we have searched everywhere in this area. The neighbors have had search parties out, but no one has seen Evan or that carriage, and what's to be done now, I'm sure I don't know."

"Bow Street Runners," said Lord Ashby suddenly, and the others looked at him blankly.

"Of course!" cried Violet. "How clever of you, Lord Ashby, to think of it! We shall call in the Runners and if anyone can find Evan, they can."

Lord Ashby blushed again at Violet's praise and Penelope's grateful expression. "No problem at all. I shall post back to London tonight and go around to Bow Street as soon as I arrive. One more day and we can have the Runners looking for the boy."

Penelope stretched out her hand to him. "How very good of you, sir. How can we ever thank you?"

Quite overcome by her gratitude, Ashby took her hand and bowed over it. "Happy to be of service, ma'am."

"That is most kind of you, Ashby," said a voice from the doorway, "but I assure you that there is no need to go to such desperate lengths."

The startled group in the drawing room looked up to see Lord Hartford surveying them sardonically. As his words sank in, Violet flushed angrily.

"Indeed you might think there is no such need, Lord Hartford, but we do. It is a matter of great consequence to us to find my nephew."

"Your nephew?" he asked, obviously taken aback. "The boy is your nephew?"

"He is," she replied. "And I should like to know how you came to know that there *is* a boy, sir."

The others looked at him accusingly, even Lord

Ashby. "Dash it all, yes, Alistair," he said. "*I* didn't know of any boy. How came you to?"

Lord Hartford looked at him quizzically. "Yes, it is a bit surprising that you did not know, Ash. I should have thought from your intimacy with Lady Danby that she would have told you everything."

"My intimacy with Lady Danby? Well, if that ain't the outside of enough, Alistair! I just met the lady and you begin to talk of my intimacy with her. Dashed if I don't think you're getting queer in the attic. He is not usually quite so rag-mannered," he said in a slightly lowered voice to Penelope. "Improves upon acquaintance."

Despite her distress at the situation, Violet could scarcely suppress a giggle at the mystified expression on Lord Hartford's face as he stared at his friend. Abandoning the riddle for the moment, he turned to Mrs. Crawford.

"I feel that I should warn you, Mrs. Crawford, that I fear that you are about to have more guests descend upon you."

"Why, who else would be coming?" asked Violet, astonished.

He smiled gently at her. "I was a trifle delayed getting my carriage prepared for the journey after I saw you and Lord Ashby departing from London, so happy in one another's company. I had some business of my own to complete."

He dangled his quizzing glass thoughtfully for a moment before he spoke again. "I am quite certain that I recognized two of the vehicles that I passed on the road. One of them belongs to my aunt and the other to my cousin, Lord Granville."

Violet stared at him blankly. "Whyever would they be coming here? You must have been mistaken."

"I think not," he smiled. "As to why they are coming, we shall know that directly, I should imagine."

"And if I may ask without being rude," Violet said suddenly. "May I ask what brought you here, Lord Hartford?"

"I wondered when you would think to ask that, Lady Danby. Your note to my aunt stated that you had an emergency here and, as your friend, I naturally wished to place myself at your disposal, even though I apprehended that you already had a cavalier in Lord Ashby."

Lord Ashby flushed again to the roots of his blond hair. "Dash it all, Alistair, not a cavalier. Lady Danby . . . needed help. Just did my part."

Lord Hartford's expression darkened. "Just doing your part, eh, Ash? I suppose that is not surprising after the time you two have spent together." He took a step toward Lord Ashby, who retreated again to a safer position behind the sofa, taking Penelope with him.

"Pray do not make yourself ridiculous, Lord Hartford," Violet snapped. "Lord Ashby merely did what any gentleman would have done."

Lord Hartford did not reply, but stared instead at Penelope, who was clutching Evan's silver snuff-box in her hand and looking at him with frightened eyes. He could see that the box was something of a talisman to her, for she stroked it

195

unconsciously. His expression began to lighten and a gleam appeared in his eye as he turned to look at Violet.

"I believe that I begin to understand . . . Miss Carlton," he said, bowing.

Mrs. Crawford had failed to take in any of the conversation going forth around her from the time Lord Hartford had mentioned that she would have at least two more guests coming. Her mind had gone immediately to the practical, housewifely questions of refreshments and bedrooms for at least four unexpected guests. Turning to Lord Hartford distractedly, she asked, "Are you quite sure that they were coming here, my lord?"

He bowed to her. "Quite sure, Mrs. Crawford."

As though to prove his point there was a brisk knock at the front door. Mrs. Crawford shook her head and walked toward the kitchen. "I must speak to Cook," she murmured. "I wonder if we have any partridges put back."

Chapter Nineteen

The door swung open to reveal Lord Granville, who raised his quizzing glass to his eye and surveyed the scene before him with obvious interest. Seeing Violet, he moved forward to take her hand.

"My Dear Lady Danby, I cannot tell you how shocked I was to learn from my aunts that your nephew had been kidnapped. I came at once to offer my services to you. You have only to command me."

"That is very kind of you, Lord Granville, and I am most grateful. I should like to make you known to my aunt, Mrs. Serena Crawford and my sister Penelope," Violet replied, glaring at Lord Hartford.

"Your servant, ladies," said Lord Granville gracefully, taking the hand of each of them in turn. "I am more distressed than I can tell you about your son," he remarked to Penelope. "I assure you that I shall leave no stone unturned in my effort to help you. I can only wish that I had known earlier that Evan had a son." He looked reproachfully at Violet. "I had no idea that there was another heir."

"That is quite an interesting statement, Bevil," remarked Lord Hartford thoughtfully, "and very touching, I am sure."

"What do you mean by that remark?" asked Lord Granville angrily. "I do not like your tone, Hartford."

"Lord Ashby was just suggesting that we call in the Bow Street Runners, Bevil," said Lord Hartford casually, ignoring his question.

"Yes, and you were just saying that such a step would not be necessary," interjected Violet hotly. "And I would very much like to know what you meant by that!"

A peremptory knocking resounded through the house, interrupting her.

"I daresay my aunts have arrived," said Lord Hartford pleasantly. "That sounded a great deal like Aunt Maria's cane at the door."

Penelope cast a frightened glance at her sister and shrank closer to Lord Ashby, who stood next to her protectively.

The dowager swept into the drawing room, a formidable figure in her black pelisse and bonnet, and Lady Dora bobbed along cheerfully in her wake. Seeing Violet, she hurried over and embraced her. "My dear child, I do apologize to you for bursting in upon you like this, but we were both so concerned by your note that we decided we simply must come and see for ourselves what could be done to help you."

"Stuff!" exclaimed the dowager. "I don't know why you came, Dora, but I came to find out about the St. Clair diamonds and here I shall stay until I do." As though to emphasize her point, she sat down deliberately on a small sofa, her black skirts billowing about her, looking as though she had every intention of becoming a permanent fixture in the drawing room.

Ignoring Lady Granville, Violet addressed herself again to Lord Hartford. "I would like to know, sir, why you think it is not necessary to send for the Bow Street Runners."

"The Bow Street Runners!" exclaimed the dowager, affronted. "I should think that Alistair does have more sense than to call in the Runners! This is a family matter and will be settled within the family!"

Violet turned to her impatiently. "We are not discussing the diamonds, Lady Granville. We are—"

The dowager cut her short and thumped her cane against the floor. "You may not wish to discuss them, my girl, but I assure you that you are going to. I did not drive all this distance merely to have a look at you and your family. Now let us make short work of it and tell me where they are."

The others had listened to her with varying degrees of astonishment and dismay. It was Lord Hartford's voice that cut through the general babble, however.

"I would suggest, Aunt, that you address yourself to Bevil if you wish to know where the diamonds are."

Bevil grew pale as he stared at Lord Hartford and then his lip curled as he turned toward his aunt. "We all know very well what happened to the diamonds," he replied in a sneering voice. "My precious cousin stole them and lost them at the gaming table."

"Bevil! How dare you say such a thing in my presence!" said the dowager in an awful voice.

"We all know it's true," he said, "but we all tiptoe around the truth so that there will be no scandal about the Granville name. What rot! Evan lost the diamonds gambling and replaced them with paste substitutes. Why, he even gave his bride a ring and a brooch made of paste. Quite the little gentleman, our Evan!"

"That is not true!" replied Penelope hotly, clutching the snuffbox so tightly that her knuckles were white. "Evan would never have taken anything that was not his! Never! And, as for saying that he would give his bride a ring of paste—you must be mad to say such things, Lord Granville!"

The dowager, who had taken no notice of her before, turned to stare approvingly at Penelope, who still stood glaring at Lord Granville, her slender shoulders heaving with anger.

"Exactly! Very well said, my girl," applauded Lady Granville. "I don't know who you are, but I see that you knew my son."

Lord Hartford took Penelope by the hand and led her gently to Lady Granville. "Allow me, Aunt, the pleasure of presenting to you Lady Danby."

The dowager was, for once, shocked into silence and could merely stare at Penelope, who made the briefest of curtsies and retreated to stand between her aunt and Lord Ashby.

"And now," said Lord Hartford amiably, "while everyone is momentarily quiet, I propose that we continue our discussion of the diamonds." He turned to Bevil once more and his voice grew less friendly. "And now, Bevil, I repeat, would you like to explain to our aunt where the diamonds are?"

"I've already told you, Hartford, and we both know it to be true." Lord Granville stared at him balefully, but with no effect.

"It won't wash, you know, Bevil," said Lord Hartford quietly.

"I don't know what you mean!" blustered Bevil, staring wildly around the room at the startled expressions of the others.

"Did you know, Bevil, that Lawson, your man of business, had been to see me?" inquired Hartford casually, almost absently.

Lord Granville looked suddenly more alert. "Why did Lawson want you?" he asked nervously.

"He wanted to discuss a few matters concerning the estate," Lord Hartford replied.

"I call that damned impertinence!" shouted Bevil. "What colossal cheek to discuss my affairs with someone else."

"You must forgive him," said Lord Hartford gently. "He has worked for the Granvilles for forty years, you know, and it cut him to the heart to see that you were planning to sell off all of the property that was not entailed. He was merely wanting me to speak to you about it."

The dowager stared at Bevil in amazement. "Cut up the property? Whatever for, Bevil? And you cannot do it yet, at any rate, for the estate is not yet settled."

Lord Hartford nodded in agreement. "That is the only thing that his prevented his doing so, Aunt. I am afraid that Bevil is at Point Non Plus and it was only your husband's untimely death that saved his groats. He had already mortgaged or sold everything of his own."

Bevil started to protest, but apparently thought better of it and lapsed into gloomy silence.

"After Lawson came to see me at Hartford Park a few weeks ago, I began to make a few inquiries of my own," he continued, "and I discovered, Bevil, that you had been in Dun territory for some time. In fact, although you had sold everything possible that you owned yourself, you still did not have sixpence to scratch yourself with until shortly before the Granville diamonds disappeared. Then, magically, just a few weeks before that, you had enough of the ready to pay most of your gaming debts. Quite interesting, I thought."

"Did you, indeed?" sneered Lord Granville.

"Yes," replied Lord Hartford imperturbably. "Particularly when it occurred to me that Lady Danby's jewels might be paste and I discovered that the brooch, at least, most definitely was. I had suspected as much, but once I could survey it closely myself, I was certain."

Penelope's face fell. "But how could that be?" she asked. "Evan would not have given me a trumpery ring and told me that it was a family heirloom."

"Not intentionally," he replied. "So far as Evan knew, the ring and brooch were authentic, and I should imagine that Bevil could tell us precisely how they came to be in Evan's possession."

"He gave them to Evan," answered Penelope promptly, "and told him that Lady Granville had sent them for me."

The dowager swelled visibly. "You dared to do such a thing, Bevil St. Clair? Why, you tried to hoodwink us all!"

"And he almost did so, Aunt, substituting paste jewels for the real ones and blaming their loss on Evan. In fact, he would have succeeded nicely, if it had not been for Lady Danby's sister Violet, who decided to come to London in her place. She managed to stir things up so much that a number of things came to the surface that otherwise might have escaped us. I should say that we owe her a great deal."

The dowager looked at Violet with new interest. "So it would seem. I like you better now than I did earlier, my girl, but I tell you frankly that I like your sister better. I like the way she stood up for my son."

She turned back to Lord Hartford. "But tell me, Alistair, what would Bevil have done if Evan had lived to come back and deny that he had taken the diamonds?"

His eyes narrowed. "Bevil was playing a very deep game, Aunt. I am very much afraid that Evan would have met with an unfortunate accident very soon after returning to England. Bevil could not afford for the truth to come out and he was being bled quite regularly by Sir Reginald Hawke, unless I miss my guess."

"Sir Reginald!" gasped Violet. "Of course! He had the real diamonds that Bevil had given him to pay his debts, and he used them to blackmail him."

"Sir Reginald is quite a greedy fellow," remarked Lord Hartford, "and blackmail, as we well know, is his specialty." Violet blushed and looked away, remembering how she had lost Penelope's brooch. "Lord Granville, however, was quite the fattest pigeon he had snared. When Evan died so conveniently and Bevil stood next in the succession, I imagine that it did not take Sir Reginald long to realize how much he stood to gain when Bevil inherited. And I am sorry to say, Aunt, that I suspect that he helped to hurry my uncle from this world to the next."

The dowager gasped and Bevil turned chalk white. "You cannot prove a thing, Hartford! That is an outrageous charge!"

"No, I suspect that I cannot prove that, Bevil, for as yet I have not been able to turn up any proof. If it is any comfort to you, I feel certain that Sir Reginald, and not you, was the driving force in my uncle's death."

Upon hearing that Lord Hartford could not prove his charge, Bevil had relaxed perceptibly, but Hartford's next words made him stiffen again.

"This time, however, the two of you have overreached yourselves, Bevil. For I can prove your complicity in this present crime."

Violet caught her breath as everyone else stared at Lord Hartford. "Oh, no! You are speaking of Evan! They are the ones that have stolen Evan away!"

She looked at Lord Granville in horror, her hands clenched. "You knew that my sister was Lady Danby and it was you that read my letters and learned about Evan and now you have taken him away!" Penelope began to cry softly and Lord

204

Ashby patted her hand akwardly.

The dowager looked confused. "Why is she speaking of Evan? Evan has been dead these three years."

Lord Hartford answered her gently. "She is speaking of Evan's son, Aunt."

Lady Granville grew white and Lady Dora hurried forward with the smelling salts, but was waved away. "Tell me," she said in a strained voice, suddenly looking much older. "What has happened to my grandson?"

"He has been kidnapped by Bevil and Sir Reginald," said Lord Hartford. "Sir Reginald's valet overheard Violet buying a toy for her three-year-old nephew and that alerted them. Bevil read some of the letters that Violet kept in her dressing table and confirmed that there was indeed such a boy. Of course, once Sir Reginald realized that the boy existed, he knew that he must be gotten rid of, and forced Bevil to assist him in the matter. Bevil was quite anxious to retain his title, of course, but a little squeamish about murder."

"How can you speak so calmly about his murder?" cried Violet, her eyes blazing. "How can you be so completely unfeeling?"

"You can prove nothing!" said Bevil, his eyes wide and frightened.

"And I assure you that I can," said Lord Hartford in a harsh voice. He walked from the drawing room to the front door and called into the darkness. "Jem, come in here, please, and bring Evan in with you."

In the open doorway appeared a solid young man

holding a small boy by the hand.

"Evan!" cried Penelope, holding out her arms.

"Mama, I'm home," he called, running to her. "And I've had an adventure with Jem. He came and got me from the two bad men and he drew their corks for 'em. He's going to show me how, Mama. It was ever so exciting, but I missed you."

"Oh, I missed you, too," she murmured, her golden head bent low over his as she held him close.

Unexpectedly, the dowager sniffed loudly and said crossly, "Find me my handkerchief, Dora. This autumn dampness is bringing on a cold." Hiding a smile, Lady Dora handed her a small square of lace and the Dowager blew her nose majestically.

"Why, that's Jem Howard," said Lord Ashby in sudden recognition. "Spent some time with Gentleman Jackson. Very handy with his fives."

"Quite right, Ash," replied his friend, smiling. "Very handy indeed, which is why I employed him to come down here and keep an eye on the boy."

"But how did you know, Lord Hartford?" asked Violet in wonder. "I know now that Lord Granville must have read my letters from Penelope and discovered that she had a son, but—"

Lord Granville, who had collapsed into the nearest chair when Jem walked in with the boy, spoke up bitterly. "Hartford was right. It was that damned man of Hawke's. He heard you buying toys for your nephew when you were out and what must he do but run home and tell his master. Then there was the devil to pay, for he knew from me that your sister was the real Lady Danby. I read your letters to make sure."

Violet ignored him and looked straight at Lord Hartford. "But how did you know, sir? I said nothing to you."

"When I set about making inquiries about Bevil, I also investigated you and your family. I found that you did indeed have a sister and that there was a boy who lived here. However," he hesitated a moment, "I thought that Evan was your son, and I still believed you to be Lady Danby. Once I suspected what Bevil's game was, I knew that the boy would have to be protected."

She looked at him wonderingly. "Then you thought you were protecting my son?"

He nodded stiffly. Violet smiled at him softly. "Thank you, Lord Hartford."

They drew a little apart from the group and stood smiling at one another.

She held out her hand to him and he took it eagerly, drawing her closer to him. "Am I to be forgiven then?" he asked, looking down into her eyes. The intensity of his gaze shook her and she stared studiously at his cravat.

"There is nothing to forgive, sir. Indeed, I know all too well that I am the one who should be asking forgiveness for my masquerade and the trouble . . ."

Violet broke off suddenly, quite losing her train of thought as Hartford kissed first one eyebrow, then the other.

"I could consider forgiveness," he said softly, kissing her cheek, "if you could consider becoming my wife."

Violet found that it was quite impossible to consider anything, indeed to breathe, as he pulled her to him and pressed his lips firmly against her own.

It was the ringing voice of Lady Granville that called them back to reality. "Alistair Granville! Of all the rag-mannered, unseemly behavior! And in front of my grandson to boot!" Her reprimand delivered, she transferred her attention back to Evan and his mother.

"I do not think that your sister need fear my aunt," remarked Lord Hartford. "Aunt Maria seems to be quite taken with both Lady Danby and her grandson. As does Lord Ashby, I might add."

He spoke no more than the truth, for the dowager sat regarding her newfound relatives with a benevolent eye and Lord Ashby gazed down at Penelope, adoration written clearly upon his face.

"I hope that you are not too cut up that Ash is so taken by your sister," remarked Lord Hartford casually.

"I shall make a recovery," Violet replied. "I had my hopes, of course," she said, dimpling, "but I shall bear my sorrow bravely. They do call me the Merry Widow, you know."

"Well do I know it, Miss Carlton. All too well. But if I have my way, my dearest, and I shall, you know, you may be as merry as you wish as Lady Hartford, but it will be a very long while before you are a widow."

She smiled contentedly and snuggled into the arm he had tucked around her. "High-handed, odious man," she murmured, chuckling.